ABOUT THE AUTHOR

Laurie Avadis is a keen athlete, artist, photographer, and a musician (he routinely gigs with his band, The Nightingale Experience after spending about 250 years as lead singer of The Last Postman) – but writing has been his definitive mode of expression from an early age. He is a practicing family lawyer with his own firm in Camden Town, passionate about justice for children, and lives in Surrey with his wife, three cats and one tiny fish which is immortal. Ex is his first book.

D1385677

EX

LAURIE AVADIS

unbound

This edition first published in 2015

Unbound
4–7 Manchester Street Marylebone London w1u 2ae
www.unbound.co.uk

Grateful Acknowledgements to Wild Animals. 28 January 2010. Published by
Joomag.com

Typeset by Press Books

Art direction by Mecob

A CIP record for this book
is available from the British Library

ISBN 978-1-78352-087-9 (trade edition)
ISBN 978-1-78352-162-3 (ebook)
ISBN 978-1-78352-088-6 (limited edition)

Printed in Great Britain by Clays Ltd, St Ives plc

For my wife, Catherine

You were my almost father
and I was your nearly child

The Day Before the Day Before You Died
Laurie Avadis

Dear Reader,

The book you are holding came about in a rather different way to most others. It was funded directly by readers through a new website: **Unbound**.

Unbound is the creation of three writers. We started the company because we believed there had to be a better deal for both writers and readers. On the Unbound website, authors share the ideas for the books they want to write directly with readers. If enough of you support the book by pledging for it in advance, we produce a beautifully bound special subscribers' edition and distribute a regular edition and e-book wherever books are sold, in shops and online.

This new way of publishing is actually a very old idea (Samuel Johnson funded his dictionary this way). We're just using the internet to build each writer a network of patrons. Here, at the back of this book, you'll find the names of all the people who made it happen.

Publishing in this way means readers are no longer just passive consumers of the books they buy, and authors are free to write the books they really want. They get a much fairer return too – half the profits their books generate, rather than a tiny percentage of the cover price.

If you're not yet a subscriber, we hope that you'll want to join our publishing revolution and have your name listed in one of our books in the future. To get you started, here is a £5 discount on your first pledge. Just visit unbound.com, make your pledge and type ex555 in the promo code box when you check out.

Thank you for your support,

Dan, Justin and John
Founders, Unbound

EX

CHAPTER 1

Just before his eighth birthday, Daniel's father tried to kill him. It was a family tradition. Five o'clock one vindictive October morning his father wordlessly ushered him from the sanctuary of his bed and drove him down to the Thames at Kingston.

Daniel sat on the dank towpath sheltering under an umbrella whilst his father, M, inflated an alarmingly ragged dinghy that had been hidden under the morass of 'kit' he stored in the rear of the family car.

'Here we are,' said M, standing back to admire his efforts, his remaining strands of hair billowing in the icy wind, raindrops strafing his pate.

'Where are we?' asked Daniel.

'I am here,' M replied, lugging the dinghy awkwardly over and into the water where it landed with a splat. 'And you,' he led Daniel over to the dinghy and helped him in, 'you are in there.'

Daniel took stock for a moment. The dinghy teetered on the jagged waves, taking in an alarming quantity of water. He was dressed in his school uniform – no surprise really, since he spent every waking moment of his childhood in that uniform – it was the middle of winter, and he had no oars.

Daniel looked up at his father tearfully as he was cast out into the deluge by a single prod of M's favoured forefinger. 'I have no oars, Dad. The boat's all leaky.'

'Far too much emphasis is placed on issues such as aquatic propulsion and buoyancy,' his father bellowed. 'Be a man, Daniel.'

But Daniel did not want to be a man. He wanted to experience the kind of life normal children lived – to be pursued by a swarm of killer bees across the veld or sewing up footballs until his fingers bled in a huge windowless factory. Instead, he found himself clinging to the sides of a sinking dinghy, borne along the Thames by a racing current, soaked to the bone, unable to differentiate between river and rain.

He must have swallowed at least half his body weight in water before washing up at the lock, about half a mile downstream. The lock-keeper plucked Daniel out of the maelstrom with his spade-like hands and pumped life back into his stuttering lungs. An ambulance retrieved him and placed him, quivering, into the festering belly of Kingston Hospital where he was studiously neglected. A staff nurse who had discovered him sitting on the floor in a corridor called his father who had only just returned home, presumably to plan his funeral and thus he was repaired and restored, unquestioningly, to the care of M.

Daniel could tell immediately by his face that he had disappointed M yet again. It was not his fault, no one had shown him how to be murdered – it was no wonder that he wasn't good at it.

The incident hardened Daniel in many ways. His father spoke of further river-based experiences with great enthusiasm and even at this tender age Daniel could see that he intended to try to kill him again. On his eighth birthday Daniel gathered together his few monetary assets and made his first and perhaps wisest investment. The next time M knocked on his bedroom door on a Sunday morning, Daniel emerged already fully dressed and wearing his very own second-hand Royal Navy life vest.

CHAPTER 2

M had not always wanted to murder his son with such determined reluctance. There were times when, some might say, he had been an inherently good man.

'I am an inherently good man,' he would think to himself as he offered the train seat he had coveted to an elderly citizen, silently entreating their heart to explode before they could accept it. 'I am the best of the best,' he would think, ushering a young mother across the road ahead of him, as his right foot furtively toyed with his accelerator pedal. 'I love all of humanity,' he would declare loudly as he opened a shop door for a soiled and ungracious youth, envisioning as he did so the noise its nose would make as he slammed the door back into its face.

Who, then, was able to glimpse the inner virtues of this ostentatiously poisonous individual? His mother, Bernice? No, she had long since abandoned the cruel seas and toxic deserts of North London for a home atop the wild mountain ranges of Milton Keynes, rationalising that since there was nothing left there that was worth burning, she would be safe from the ravages of modern times. To her, M was no more than an occasional unwanted visitor, like the Hare Krishna or influenza and whilst absent, his face became vague and dissipated as if it had been drawn on tissue paper and dropped into a bowl of warm water.

Siblings? Perhaps an elder sister who swooped down from on high in times of trouble, shielding M from the ravages of the Highgate sun? Someone who could navigate through the elephantine folds of her brother's skin to the simple golden heart beating beneath? There was a sister, Bathsheba, but her exit from the familial nest had been more like a double-decker bus than an eagle. To her, life was like an out of control HGV, unconscious driver slumped over the steering wheel, careering towards her with malicious and destructive intent. Simply getting out of bed in the morning was a task of Herculean complexity, so swooping was right out of the question.

A brother then, statesman like, ushering M down a path well trodden, a virtuous figurehead, loved by all, who could find good in even the venal wasteland that was M's soul? There was a brother, Clive, who adored M, but only in the inclusive manner in which he cherished everything and everyone through the Fuzzy Felt eyes of a whisky bottle. Clive could not judge the distance between his feet and the urinal he was often found slumped over and was certainly in no fit state to assess his brother's worth.

Lost behind the chorus in the theatre of malice that played day after day in M's mind, it was Daniel who saw the good in his father. Daniel, who lay like a discarded rag doll in his father's febrile world. A trophy from a battle lost, the son after the son cherished. Daniel who loved his father with an unconditional drip drip drip, until even that tap finally ran dry through rancur and neglect.

Only M's wife had dug deep enough to trace and nurture the tiny shoots of virtue that dwelt within him amongst an impenetrable forest of brutality. But any remaining emotional attachment had been severed like the amputation of a vestigial thumb on the day she realised that she was a mermaid and M was more the devil than the deep blue sea.

CHAPTER 3

M's brother Clive was obsessed by the concept of owning a boat. He imagined a vessel borne upon a raging sea of blood, hurtling inexorably towards a gaping ventricle; it would buck and yawl whilst Neptune gouged at its shimmering bows. He knew he must build the boat with his own hands, moulding and caressing every inch until it was as sleek as red wine and invisible to the touch. He would kiss its stern with ardour and set it free upon a limitless horizon which he would navigate without blinking.

Clive's wife, Dorritt, had hoped on the night of its conception that it was the whisky bottle's idea to construct a 'seafaring vessel' in the lounge of their already cramped, semi-detached home in Dollis Hill and not her insensible spouse's, but, in the morning, work commenced.

Clive was an utter cunt. If Dorritt had any remaining doubt about his redoubtable all round cuntishness then what became known as 'the boat project', aka grounds 1–9 of her divorce petition, erased it.

'Where will this end?' his wife had asked him when, after the third week, construction of a cabin had necessitated the evacuation of 'Destiny', their irksome pet armadillo, together with their dining table and chairs.

'We will set sail for a land trodden only by the minotaur,' replied Clive.

'Stanmore?' asked his wife.

'Far beyond Stanmore to the shale fortresses, a place where acid creatures wrestle each other in the boughs of trees made of glass,' replied Clive.

There was a pause whilst his wife pondered the exotic possibilities. 'Neasden?' she asked.

*

Sharing her home with 100 plus whisky bottles at various stages of consumption and a shit-panted apoplectic drunk who used them as a mattress was pretty much what Dorritt had signed up for when she married Clive. She was aware that he had a tapestry of shortcomings and that he had suffered at the hands of a dystopian tyrant as a child but when he laughed he became the little boy that had never been vanquished. And yet, she wandered through desperate sleepless hours at night as breath percolated up through Clive's lungs with a tenacious whistle and imagined the friction of her hands around his throat; by day her friends and family had become distant aliens and laughter became as rarefied as alpine air. Had it been the project, 'Clive,' that she had fallen in love with rather than the man? How could she endure this eternal poverty of rapture?

When he was building the boat he was not drinking – it became his mistress – inching her out of her home, offering him the momentum to defy addiction, assuming the wifely role that she had never quite fulfilled, but it was satiating him whilst consuming her.

'The TV has to go,' said Clive, atop a ladder, saw in hand, wood shavings so thick on the ground around her feet that they had formed a dray. 'And the settee and the sideboard, it all has to go.'

'And what about me?' asked Dorritt. 'Where do I go?'

Clive paused from splicing and carving at a muscular section of tree to compare his craftsmanship with his marriage. With every dowel and every mitre joint, he was deconstructing the woman who had withstood the torrent of inhumanity he had rained upon her on a daily basis. With every rebate joint and stopped house joint he was stripping away another layer of the indefatigable love that had held his head over another vomitous toilet bowl and smoothed back his rat's tail fringe. He pulled an open mortise joint and a bridle joint from his leather apron pocket and inserted one into the other. They fitted perfectly, Dorritt and Clive, assembled, crafted, he was needed, she needed him. It wasn't Dorritt he wanted to sail away from but everything else and he could only do it on his own. This would be proof that his father was wrong, that he was not beyond merit, that he was not the personification of reproach.

'I have to make this journey,' said Clive. 'And what part will I play?' asked Dorritt. Her face was a passive mask, behind it were a thousand screams. 'Where will I be as you sail past the tattered cliffs of Queensbury on your way to the straits of Canons Park and beyond?'

He knew that what he would say next would determine the course their marriage would take. That it needed to be a statement of loving intent if he was to convince her that he was still her knight in argent. 'Can you smash a hole in our bedroom floor with the monkey wrench so I can stick the mast through?' asked Clive. 'And mind the Armadillo.'

*

M had not assumed a parental role in the lives of his siblings because, to them, the title parent was artifice, their words poison, their assumed task, deforestation of the young until all that remained were saplings whose growth would be distorted and grotesque. He knew that he could not protect his brother and sister from abuse any more than he could make himself visible amongst an adult world of turned heads. Whilst he had been able to lock the hurricane deep inside in order to be the father he knew he needed to be for Saul, Clive and Bathsheba lacked that resource. He saw Clive and Bathsheba as victims of war crimes to whom nature dictated he must offer solace and refuge, but these were minds damaged beyond repair by a dexterous cruelty.

Just as a cowering child he had been unable to predict where his parents would strike next, often, actually always, M found himself arriving too late to repair the damage caused to society by his elaborately deranged siblings and this time was no different. By the time M entered the front door of number 22 Venison Chase, it had become a husk, clinging to Clive's mighty vessel for support rather than simply housing it. M had decided to visit when Dorritt had finally resorted to contacting her despicable brother-in-law with a singular text message – 'I've left your fucking brother to play with his 90 ft tall mistress.'

M stood in what had once been Clive's front room and searched for a degree of sarcasm that was extreme enough for this situation before deciding that it did not exist. The boat had not been built from any specific plans, more a combination of watching *The Vikings* with Kirk Douglas, studying an Airfix model of the *Cutty Sark*, a photograph of the Battleship USS *Missouri* torn out of *Hounds and Homes* magazine, a painting of HMS *Victory* by a seven-year-old schoolchild, a beer mat upon which 'Terrence the destroyer' had drawn the battleship *Potemkin* and the face of Elvis in felt-tip pen and thirty-six viewings of the complete boxed set of *Voyage to the Bottom of the Sea*. This, coupled with a four week entry-level carpentry course and a copy of the *Rubber Dinghies can be Fun* annual from 1963 had been the blueprint for the creation of what was most likely the largest seafaring wooden potato ever assembled by a human being.

'It's my boat,' said Clive. 'I made it.'

'A boat,' said M, standing back as far as he could to try to gain some limited degree of perspective.

'What,' tried M and then, 'how.' 'It must be eight and a half miles from here to the Thames, assuming you don't just intend to bob around on the Brent Reservoir and even moving this giant wooden turd to the end of the garden would be impossible given that it currently resides inside a semi-detached fucking house.'

'We have a plan,' replied Clive, smiling.

'We,' said M, 'tell me you haven't involved our mutant, Benzedrine-soaked, loony loop sister in yet another episode of the car crash of your existence?'

'It's a really good plan,' said Clive.

*

When M, Bathsheba and Clive had been little more than lower case vowels, they had been able to escape to the park alone for a few hours whilst their parents were engaging in their preferred callisthenic leisure activity of hacking chunks out of each other. They had been sitting in the grass watching other children play around the swings and climbing frames when a little boy of about Bathsheba's age, with ebulliently golden locks, came and sat next to them.

'Why aren't you playing?' he asked no one in particular.

'Don't know how,' replied Bathsheba.

'Why don't you try, it's fun,' said the little boy, taking her hand and pulling her towards the sandpit.

'It's only fun because you know you are going to be allowed to do it again,' said M. 'Otherwise it's a punishment.'

*

Sonja and Batty Sherman had been trying to sell 20 Venison Chase even before the boat project was conceived, living as they did in a property adjoining that of a man who regarded a night pitched face down in their rose bushes wearing clothing whose fibres were held together by DNA and excrement to be 'a nice little soiree'. Efforts to interest buyers were hampered by the skip full of whisky bottles in their neighbour's drive and the philharmonic cacophony of crapulous abuse issuing from next door at random times of the night and day. They sought resolution through the courts, the council, even the local scout leader was approached in a last desperate throw of the dice, but Dorritt would always intervene, committing once more to tame her savage spouse. Everyone was charmed by Dorritt. When the screaming ended and the sawing commenced, their objections were moribund – they were defeated, they removed the 'For Sale' board, quadruple-glazed their windows, wore surgically implanted wax earplugs and learned sign language.

*

On an ultramarine Saturday morning, nearer to August than any other month, Sonja was peering out of her kitchen window when her eyes fell upon something which caused her no little perturbation. She turned momentarily – Batty was sitting at the kitchen table, enthralled in the freshly ironed *Times* and Sonja gained his attention by lovingly throwing a half full coffee mug at his head.

'Outside,' she signed. 'Big. Really big.'

'A bus,' signed Batty.

'Not a bus, bigger, swings – like a –' Sonja grabbed for the signing dictionary. 'Like a giant apple on a rope.'

'A giant orange on a rope?' signed Batty imaginatively.

Sonja glanced nervously back at the window, 'not a giant orange you moron – how many giant oranges have you seen? They use this when they build, it's made of steel, it swings and smashes.' She searched forlornly for the sign but there was nothing like it...

Batty put down his paper, sighed, parked his reading glasses and joined Sonja at the window.

'A wrecking ball,' he said.

'Yes,' said Sonja. 'At last, a –'

*

Bathsheba, sister of Clive and M, had never driven a crane before nor wielded a wrecking ball but she did both with gusto and not a little flair. Sonja and Batty's home quickly resembled the ruined heart of Stalingrad in 1942, which allowed Bathsheba to concentrate on gently demolishing 22 Venison Chase without damaging the glorious craft which lay within.

*

'Now what,' said M, standing in the steaming rubble of Dorritt and Clive's former abode, staring at his embracing siblings.

'Now we tow it to the Thames,' replied Clive.

'It will fit down all the main roads – I've measured them,' said Bathsheba.

'It may fit down all of the main roads if there are no cars parked on them,' replied M. 'But there are going to be parked cars. What then?'

'We destroy them,' said Bathsheba, walking back down the street where she had, much earlier that week, under the cover of darkness, casually concealed under an ill-fitting tarpaulin 33.4 tons of Sherman tank and a boat trailer.

*

M had formed the view, after some deliberation, that turning his sister, whose connection to reality was at best euphemistic, loose on the streets of London with a fully armed Sherman tank was a little bit, well, dangerous. Furthermore, he reasoned, association with said Sherman tank towing, as it did, a giant wooden amphibious potato might not, in the eyes of The Metropolitan Police, his albeit forward-thinking employers (who were, when all was said and done, generally risk-averse when it came to acts of wanton carnage), represent conduct which was likely to enhance his already wafer-thin career prospects.

'Who suddenly appointed you the arbiter of reason?' asked Clive. 'You pose more of a risk to society than any giant weaponised amphibious root vegetable as far as I am concerned. We always knew where we were with dad. You did something wrong, you were punished, you did something right, you were punished more; with Bathsheba and me, each slap was like a nail driven into a tree branch. We were split, warped, degraded; but it was as if you became all the more impregnable.'

'I have fathered Saul with none of our imperfections,' replied M.

'You think he can't see what his father is? He sees. We all see. My crutch is the bottle, Bathsheba's is the pharmacy, what's yours? Your son? Have you ever asked yourself what the world would look like for you, for all of us, if that crutch was kicked away?'

It was not a question which M had posed to himself. Like all those that love one person with blind and absolute devotion he could not imagine what he might be capable of doing to the person he held accountable for their loss.

M agreed to rendezvous with Clive and Bathsheba at Shad Thames, where the 'Pool of London' meant that the river was at its deepest. He had been listening in to the police radio as the tank weaved its path of destruction through the streets of London, writing off innumerable vehicles and threatening an over eager traffic warden in West Finchley with extreme prejudice. A task force of five police attack helicopters, three hundred officers in riot gear and a battalion of the Royal Scottish Dragoon Guards had been poised to intercept but had been stood down in a dispute over overtime pay. The union representative for the Metropolitan Police Officers Federation described the eventual financial settlement some twelve weeks later as 'a momentous development in the landscape of the future calculation of productivity incentive payments,' although he regretted the resultant 500 fold increase in crime during this period of "creative police inactivity".'

*

Once it was launched on the Thames, M was concerned that 'El Patata de la Redención' (The Potato of Redemption) might be something of a death-trap, however he had sworn to himself as a child that if he could not protect his younger siblings then he would, at least, perish with them and it was with this glowing endorsement that he stepped on to the bow of the boat.

'Where now?' asked M, expecting perhaps a quick foray over to Canvey Island, which would get him back in time for the dinners he had planned for 6pm, 7pm, 8pm, 9pm and 11.30pm that evening. He had noticed that the area of deck where they stood was at once convex and concave – it was not a vessel which was exactly streamlined.

'Chia Daakwokweyeh,' replied Clive, as if M would obviously know where this was, without need for further explanation.

'North Sentinel Island in the Indian Ocean,' said Bathsheba with unusual clarity. 'The only island on the planet which has never been explored or influenced by Western civilisation.'

'Populated by the Sentinelese – who have greeted all previous visitors with extreme and relentless violence and whose society is believed to be replete with adultery and sudden death,' explained Clive.

'So I won't need my passport then,' said M.

*

Clive showed M to the cockpit of the La patata de la Redención and proudly took him through the various empty square and round holes in the instrumentation panel where the complex equipment required to navigate and control the boat would have sat if he had purchased it.

'Correct me if I am wrong, but isn't the Indian Ocean about nine thousand miles away?' asked M.

'Ten thousand miles,' replied Clive.

'And how do you hope to get there?' asked M.

'We have a steering wheel and a big sail and a tractor engine and a rudder,' replied Clive.

'And maps,' added Bathsheba. 'We bought some nice maps.'

'And we have this,' said Clive, taking off his right shoe and showing M the small compass concealed within the heel.

'Just in case you do actually get this thing out of the Thames and on to the open sea, do you actually have the quantity of food and fresh water you need for a journey of this...'

M could see his brother was beginning to lose the sheen of confidence which had illuminated his face since M had first seen him earlier that day. Clive's hands were beginning to shake again as the ache for the bottle was returning to his gut.

'You never share our vision, M, you never see the world through our eyes,' said Clive.

'Why must we always be defeated?' asked Bathsheba.

M knew nothing of the sea or of how the world might appear through the eyes of his siblings but he knew all about destination. He thought about Saul, now at home, playing in the peripheral presence of M's wife. He wondered if his son experienced their symbiotic relationship in the way that M did. Was he too reliant on this young child to maintain his structural integrity against the screaming hordes circling and shooting flaming arrows towards the crumbling edifice of his sanity? He could not bring himself to accept that he was. But, all the same, M found himself yearning to have Saul by his side again to restore his equilibrium.

A student of calculus, he decided that a purely mathematical approach was required in order to objectively assess the risk that his siblings would indeed circumnavigate the globe:

$$h(x) - 3 + 29 = x$$

h (giant floating militarised tuber) (x) (bollocks-for-brains siblings) – 3 (navigating 10,000 nautical miles of cruel and unpredictable ocean using only the compass in the heel of a pair of Clarks Pathfinder shoes) + 29 (reality) = x (not a fucking prayer)

'Carpe shitting diem, bruv,' said M.

CHAPTER 4

Nightingale Fleeertch (pronounced like the noise that cats make when they are coughing up a fur ball) had been working on the Thames flood barrier as deputy assistant operations manager for just over two years. In that time he had calculated the mean average level of neap tides from 1899 to the present day, accidentally killed a swan with a remote controlled helicopter and learned to speak Volapük, a language invented in 1879 and to his knowledge spoken by no one else in the entire world. It had been nothing but a roller coaster of near death thrills and spills. Away from work, he had watched the film *Flood*, in which an Armageddon-sized tsunami engulfs and destroys the Thames flood barrier, one hundred and fifty-eight and 1/8th times. On the commencement of the one hundred and fifty-ninth viewing his girlfriend had picked up the DVD player and wordlessly Frisbeed it out of her flat window without opening it, along with his toothbrush, underwear and shoes. There was every chance that if she had caught him he would have been next, but he was not sorry about this denouement. She had recently confided in him that she would rather her lungs were ripped from her chest by a pack of rabid hyenas than become the next Mrs Fleeertch, so he had suspected that the relationship had lost something of its original sparkle.

Standing on the barrier's central observation deck, Nightingale picked up the high powered binoculars through which he was expected to survey the Thames for possible signs of 'a threat to the security and operational integrity of water displacement systems/resources'.

He inspected the stains on his brown(ish) tie through the long-range precision lenses – chilli chicken Tung-rymbai, stuffed eggplant, loft drip, goat intestine and woad, and that was only in the last seven days. He inhaled for what felt like a month, sighed languorously and turned his attention with huge reluctance to the Thames – the vapid shit streak that trailed its fetid intestines through the heart of the glorious city of London. What water-related wonderment awaited him this fine day? A seagull with a cyst on its arse? A barge full of slurry that had strayed minutely off route? A giant wooden potato headed directly for them on a collision course? He dropped his binoculars and fumbled for his radio transmitter.

*

'We have entered the Straits of Messina and we must defeat Charybdis and Scylla or perish where we stand,' shrieked Bathsheba, grabbing the lank wire wool which hung apologetically from her skull and pulling it out in bloodied clumps.

'It's the Thames barrier,' said M, 'not a giant armour-plated fish sucking down boats and eating their passengers whole – if the City of London Corporation had tried to install one of those it would never have got past the planning stage.'

M could see that Clive was focusing and refocusing his addled pupils upon the distant silver fingertips of London's flood defences. His mind was trying to identify what way up he was, and was not exactly functioning as a precision instrument. Residing within the four walls of Clive's skull was a landscape replete with unfettered torment – the tiny flame that his father lit and fanned had become a forest fire that had engulfed reason. He was agony, he belonged to mania, he was owned by fear. This was the defeat his father had engendered.

M reached out and took Clive's face in his black leather-gloved hands, squeezing just a little bit harder than necessary. 'Cut out the low resolution thinking and concentrate. You and Princess Leila over there couldn't navigate this thing to the end of my prick, let alone traverse the globe. Let's empty the bilge, secure the forecastle to a cleat with a lanyard, park this pile of shit by the side of the river and start again – there will be other dreams, brother, other horizons.'

Clive flinched out of M's grasp, batting his hands away with archaic wrath. 'Listen you glutted fuckmaggot, this is the dream – this, nothing else. Don't you dare, don't you dare have the audacity to pretend that you understand me, you don't have the moral compass. You have the empathetic capacity of a dung beetle. You stood there while our father stamped and stamped on anything that Bathsheba and I could have called an aspiration. You watched him abbreviate our childhoods into no more than a footnote.'

'I was a child myself.'

'You were never a child, M, not close to it.'

'I couldn't have stopped him – he couldn't stop himself,' said M with unaccustomed defensiveness.

'You could have tried, M,' replied Clive. 'Just that and no more and we would have seen that someone cared just a tiny bit, that we were children who had some intrinsic value. He swallowed us whole, he taught you rage and that's where you escaped to, but all we learned was submission. We were vacated – voided. So don't talk to me about dreams, M – I could not function as an adult – I was goaded by my wife and her fucking forgiveness, it made me sick – the worse I behaved towards her, the more she forgave and I detested her for that and disgusted myself. I flagellated our marriage until it was a blood-soaked corpse. This boat is all I am – it is all your sister is, and if she says that the Thames is blocked by a giant sea serpent then I see it too and if it is in our way then we will attack it and destroy it.' He pushed M aside and held Bathsheba – her arms stuck out like a scarecrow which slowly, stiffly, fell around and about her brother, her right hand remaining, as ever, in a fist. Human contact stung her, she was not constructed to accommodate it.

'Will you use the weapon?' she asked Clive, whilst staring fixedly forwards.

'We have no choice,' he whispered.

'Then I will fetch the sheep,' she replied.

*

'Either there is an imminent threat to security or there isn't, Fleeertch. I would have thought that even you...' The voice of Mr Grobe, the operations manager, struck out at his subordinate through the walkie-talkie.

'Well, Sir, there appears to be some kind of medieval catapult device that has been erected on the top of the giant floating potato,' replied Fleeertch.

'Your job is hanging by an imperceptible thread at this point, Fleeertch, I just wanted you to know that,' said Grobe, 'no pressure.'

'They seem to be loading the device with...' Fleeertch adjusted his binoculars. 'For the love of God, this cannot be happening.'

*

'You absolutely, categorically, are not going to launch a sheep at the Thames flood barrier,' shouted M, after Clive had uncovered a giant catapult on the top deck of the potato, ratcheted it back into a loading position and Bathsheba had emerged from the lower decks with half a dozen sheep on dog leads.

'I agree with you,' said Clive, 'using sheep like this as ammunition' – the sheep stared up at him plaintively, not enjoying all these references to sheep being used as projectiles – 'would be quite futile.' A wave of relief fell upon the sheep and they sighed collectively.

'Which is why we need to set them on fire first,' said Bathsheba.

*

'You say you are being bombarded by burning sheep?' said Grobe.

'That's what I just said,' screamed Fleeertch, ducking as a lamb fizzed past his ear and exploded through the window of the observation deck.

'Right, meet me on the war bridge,' said Grobe.

'Where's that?' asked Fleeertch as a flaming sheep bounced into the central flood barrier, turning it into a volcano. 'I didn't know we had one.'

'It's the room between the coat cupboard and the men's toilet,' said Grobe.

'I thought that was the women's toilet,' shouted Fleeertch.

'That's right, the government have militarised a women's toilet,' replied Grobe. 'Doesn't it make you proud to be British?'

*

Grobe, and Grobe's face, set permanently into a contemptuous jeer, opened the door to the women's toilet, which was now illuminated in red light as if it had been rehoused between his quivering, disparaging lips. One of the cubicles had been converted into a ready room and in the second, a panel had been lowered just above the cistern to reveal a radar screen, two keyholes and an extensive selection of toilet ducks.

Grobe had worn the same green corduroy trousers to work since the early nineties when his previous pair were ripped asunder whilst he was dangled by them over the side of Waterloo Bridge. Short of a similar subordinate-driven debasement he would be wearing this current pair until he carked. He delved into a pocket which was used to a good degree of delving and, removing two important looking keys, he placed one into Fleeertch's quivering fingers.

'We have to insert and turn at the same time. That will target and launch the peace device,' explained Grobe eagerly.

'The peace device?' asked Fleeertch.

'The weapons grade, plutonium-tipped, nuclear warhead-equipped attack torpedo,' replied Grobe, his perfectly cuboid head swivelling back and forth on his anglepoise neck. 'It's the only way to protect London from the threat posed by this,' he pointed at the potato-shaped blip on the radar from which emanated smaller, sheep-shaped blips, at regular intervals.

'I hope you will forgive me for asking, Sir,' asked Fleeertch, sure that he would not, 'but won't the devastating conflagration resulting from the explosion of a nuclear warhead, albeit a peaceful one, in the middle of the Thames, have a more negative effect on London than a few combustible sheep?'

'What can you see on this radar, Fleeertch?' asked Grobe, pointing at the landmass on either side of river.

'Woolwich, Sir?' asked Fleeertch.

'Exactly,' replied Grobe, his well-furnished eyebrows scuttling back and forwards across his forehead like rabid caterpillars. 'I doubt anyone will notice it's gone.'

*

Unable to rain barbarity down upon the heads of his siblings, as he would have done in most normal social situations, M had begun to form an exit plan, when he noticed a very un-flood-barrier-like protuberance had emerged and was now pointing directly at them.

'They are going to fuck us up,' said M.

'Thoughts drain down through your skull and are filtered through your harrowing world vision until everything that you see, everything you touch, is clogged with horror,' said Clive. 'Violence doesn't define everyone as it does you.'

M grabbed his brother by the shoulders and swivelled him 180 degrees so that he was precluded from loading any more sheep into the catapult and forced to look at the barrier.

'For a man who was emotionally vanquished by a tyrant as a child and has lived by a creed of sadistic self indulgence, you are insufferably proud. It is the kind of pride, however, that does not stand up to any form of scrutiny. That,' M pointed at the huge gun barrel which was now surrounded by red and green flashing lights, 'that is about to bring about a small but not insignificant revision to your plan to sail to the other side of the world. So I suggest you and I and our sister get the fuck out of Dodge.'

'What makes you think we want to leave?' asked Bathsheba with previously uncharted clarity.

The gun barrel began to reverberate expectantly. All but two of the lights surrounding it were now green.

17

'Surely this… boat is about aspiration, not evisceration?' asked M. 'Despite everything, all the unspeakable things we three saw, the things that bastard made us endure when we were too young to fit suffering on that scale into our hearts, even after all that, you cannot want this to be your coda.'

'You see this hand?' asked Bathsheba, waving her fisted fingers under M's nose. 'One day, it might as well have been a Tuesday, when I was five years old, our father took me to Kew Gardens. Even then I had realised that the good times were the worst, that the periods of respite from his awful revelry only allowed him to gather strength before defiling us still more. He took me into the tropical house and over to the bougainvillea, which soared up above my head in an incalculable rocket tail of crimson bound for the heavens, and he made me reach out this hand. As I touched a diaphanous flower head he closed his fingers around mine until each petal seared as if it were made from the embers of coal. He forced me to grasp until my little hand was smashed. This hand.' Tremulously she unpicked the fingers of her clenched fist one at a time with her good hand, breaking each one as she did so. Inside, hidden for thirty-six years, were the almost imperceptible remnants of a bougainvillea flower.

*

'Insert and turn the key,' snapped Grobe from the other side of the toilet cubicle.

'It isn't right, Sir,' replied Fleeertch.

'Right and wrong, they're such relative terms,' replied Grobe.

'Mr Grobe, Percival, when I was having ultrasound treatment for my kidney stone, I noticed that the nurse operating the sound wave device had turned the dial up to 5 and I asked her whether turning it up to 10 would get rid of my kidney stone. She said yes it would but that would be because my kidney would have exploded.'

'What point are you trying to make?' snarled Grobe.

'My point is – why do this? They have to run out of sheep eventually.'

'Have you ever seen one of these?' asked Grobe, removing a Ruger LCP 380 Ultra Compact Pistol from his pocket and sticking the nozzle so deeply into Fleeertch's left ear that it was within a whisker of his brain. 'This is a small calibre hand gun and this,' he pointed towards the key in Fleeertch's hand, which was doing the watusi, 'operates a very big gun. They both kill people just as dead. So what's it to be – head blown to tiny little brave pieces or key-turning cowardice?'

With one hand vaguely stemming the flow of blood from his ear, Fleeertch used the other to insert and turn the key.

'Bang bang you're dead,' said Grobe.

*

All of the lights around the barrel of the gun had turned green and it had stopped moving.

'We have to abandon this potato right now,' shouted M, grabbing his brother and sister by their wrists.

'Why protect us?' asked Clive.

'Leave us to Poseidon,' said Bathsheba, pulling loose.

'When he came home and dad wanted something to hit, something to blame, some temporary poultice to assuage the terror that this was all his life could be, I stood up and I took it for all of us,' said M.

'Why?' asked Clive.

'I don't know,' said M, turning and grabbing for his sister again.

'It wasn't enough,' said Clive, who had picked up a length of wood and planted it with no little force in the centre of M's lavishly presented forehead.

*

M half woke to find himself sharing a life raft with three sheep. He didn't like the expressions on the faces of the sheep but he could not say exactly why. He felt as if his head had been masticated by the blunt, conical, nipple-like teeth of a juvenile Tyrannosaurus rex.

Floating all around the dinghy was the burnt out wreckage of a boat. A quickly scribbled note had been shoved into his hand – it read, 'be a better man than your father'.

CHAPTER 5

But M was not a better man than his father. It was both a serious failing and a seriously difficult thing to fail at, since his father, Jonah, was an unfathomably embittered, peerlessly vicious, festering, child-hating, world-class cuntaclysm of a man.

Jonah was completely bald except for the patch of hair which grew from a huge scar on the left side of his temple. Everyone who saw the scar thought it was shaped like a penis. No one who saw the scar ever told Jonah that it was shaped like a penis but everyone thought that it was. You couldn't help it.

Jonah had inherited a cafe when his uncle died. The roof of the cafe was very low and Jonah was a very tall man. A very tall man. He could not have the ceiling raised because the cafe was built in a railway arch and it was a condition of his uncle's estate that he wasn't permitted to sell it.

Try as he might, Jonah was always cutting the top of his head on the ceiling and often wore two plasters, one crossed over the other. Eventually the plasters became a permanent fixture.

A large vein ran from just below his left eye up over his skull, under the plasters that covered the cut on his head and through the scar that was shaped like a penis, and when he was angry, the vein throbbed.

Jonah was an angry man – if you met him you knew.

It was not long after M attempted to murder Daniel for the first time that M told him he had killed Jonah with a single bullet to his brain with a gun given to him as a twelfth birthday present by his mother. They were sitting at a dining table having tea and, although they were a considerable distance away from anything that could be deemed a drowning hazard by even the most liberal construction, Daniel was wearing his life vest.

Daniel was prodding suspiciously at an egg sandwich, which might, he suspected, have been laced with some deadly bacterial agent by his father. Daniel's mother had left home a year before and only returned once a week to cut the crusts off their sandwiches and iron his underwear. When she stopped doing even this she faded away altogether like a painting that has been left in the sunshine for too long.

On this particular afternoon, M was momentarily distracted from his usual Sunday pastimes of frowning at Daniel's life vest, frowning at Daniel, frowning at the sandwiches his wife had castrated and relighting his pipe, by the burning desire to tell his son that he had offed his grandfather Mafia-style even though his grandfather was not exactly dead and was running a cafe in Hackney at the time. (It is worth noting that being dead and running a cafe in Hackney are not necessarily mutually exclusive.)

Daniel did not know what motivated M to shoot his grandfather and M would no more have confided his feelings to a bowl of cornflakes.

The whole murderous father absent mother dynamic did not provide Daniel with what could be characterised as the ideal springboard into adulthood but went some way to explain the prodigious storm cloud of shite that hung above his head for the rest of his life. A storm cloud that rained and rained.

CHAPTER 6

There are fissures at the heart of every relationship. At night if you listen carefully you can hear the sides of them groaning and grinding against each other like mighty icebergs, just above the sound of your partner snoring. You want to go back to before, when everything was new and perfect and intact but there is no before. Only after.

Even worse than Daniel's relationship with his father, and his father's relationship with his respective father, was his parents' relationship with one another, characterised as it was by the vicious carping of a psychopath and the retaliatory sniping of a woman so deluded that she had convinced herself that she was both amphibian and immortal. They had suffered more damage than most, even before his mother decided she was a mermaid and his father tried to drown him, but the cause of the first significant rupture was the boating pond incident.

You can care too much for a child. When M pushed Saul, Daniel's ex-brother, in his pram, he exuded an air of murderous propriety. Strangers were left under no misapprehension – any attempt to approach this child, no matter how cute he was, would be met with sudden and deadly justice.

Daniel's mother was little better. Entrusted with the responsibility of caring for a child whose birth had caused her to lose all equilibrium, she constructed a web of daily ticks, repetitions and habits around him which was quite impenetrable. M had witnessed the full majesty of his wife's insanity unfurl gradually like a peacock's tail. Shortly after they returned home with Saul from the maternity ward, he had found her in the attic, taking all the tiles off their roof and placing them in piles of five. Anti-psychotic medication, M discovered, was only effective when his wife actually took it.

An agreed visit to the boating pond on Hampstead Heath that Sunday was the glace cherry glistening atop a week of desperate custard. When they arrived, M took two-year-old Saul and his new radio-controlled boat to the water's edge for a maiden voyage and Daniel's mother found a park bench to observe them from. She tried to concentrate on the tottering joy of her young son but she viewed the world through eyes which appeared to have been positioned atop a tower made of jelly.

A swan and a duck approached her for food, or so she presumed, and she shooed them away.

'Do you want it?' asked the swan.

Daniel's mother looked around her. No one else appeared to have heard these avian words and yet they had been delivered with clarity.

'Do I want what?' asked Daniel's mother.

'Did she bring it?' asked the duck.

'She brought it and she wants it,' replied the swan, advancing on her.

'Look I don't know what you think I have brought but you had better leave me alone,' said Daniel's mother, shifting uncomfortably on the park bench, her eyes begging the rest the world for support it was not equipped to offer.

'I'm going to fuck you up,' said the swan.

'Fuck her up,' said the duck.

'I'm going to,' said the swan.

*

At the side of the boating pond, M held Saul by the waist as he placed his shiny red radio-controlled boat, with silken green and blue sails, into the water. The sun kissed the blue corrugated surface of the pond leaving mellifluous lipstick streaks of light, but a cloud had fallen across Saul's eyes – his little boat was being assailed from every direction by larger, more mobile vessels. M attempted to manoeuvre it into the middle of the pond, but this brought it into the path of a particularly large galleon which, rather than deviate, hit Saul's boat amidships. For a moment the little vessel bobbed in the stuttering wake of the galleon and then capsized and sank.

Saul was seized by seismic shocks of grief and jagged sobs, each one of which pained M more than the last. If he had a heart, then following the tracks of his son's tears would have been the only reliable way to locate it.

M gathered Saul up into his arms and walked him towards the car, throwing the remote control for his boat in a bin. It looked like defeat, but in M's case, that was never the end of the story.

M found the spade in his car boot where he left it for various digging related activities. Holding his son in one arm and the spade in the other, he returned to the pond but did not stop at the water's edge. He waded directly out to the galleon and although its pace was impressive in comparison to other model boats it was no match for a thirty-two stone man wielding a garden implement. The ship was cleaved in two with one single blow at which point M stopped and waited for protests from its owner. Silence and inertia had fallen upon those gathered around the boating pond in the way it did when a herd of wildebeest observe one of their number savaged and consumed by a lion. In silence there was anonymity and in anonymity there was invisibility.

M wielded the spade, smashing boat after boat into oblivion and with each blow Saul laughed and the clouds dispersed.

CHAPTER 7

It was exactly 7 years and 135 days after Saul had died, just after M had polished off his second roast chicken and was starting on a third, on what had become a somewhat typical Sunday afternoon in front of the TV, when M's wife told him that she was a mermaid.

The news that his wife was a mythical, sea-dwelling, water-breathing, sailor snaring, twenty-four carat, all singing, all dancing, denizen of the deep had been greeted with a level of sarcasm from M that was so Herculean it had reduced their already fragile relationship to weekly sandwich crust removal and underwear ironing. When she angrily demanded to know why he could not simply accept her for what she was, M had pointed out that:

(a) She had not been a mermaid for the first fifteen years of their marriage and that this Damascene revelation had only occurred after a particularly heated altercation with a parking attendant in Swanage;

(b) She had two legs rather than a fish's tail;

(c) She could not swim;

(d) Neither of her parents had been, to his knowledge, mythical aquatic creatures (although he was forced to accept that they did both lack certain basic human characteristics); and

(e) She resided in a semi-detached house in Kentish Town which, whilst raining and sodden on occasions, could not be described in any sense as a mystical underwater kingdom.

Be all that as it may, she responded, she was a mermaid and if he did not like it he could fuck off.

Their marriage had become as irretrievable and ethereal as the dreams of a battery hen. M saw the woman he had loved lose all connection with what is popularly thought of as reality, abandoning him to the parenthood of one son and the stubborn memory of a second. Their children – one for whom life had been as tenuous as the faintest touch of a cloud on a parachutist's cheek and one who refused to die.

*

Day to day suburban life was becoming increasingly challenging for Daniel's mother. Her waking thoughts were coloured by a longing for the sound and texture of the sea but as much as this thrilled her it also perplexed and petrified her. She knew that hitting a parking attendant with a spade would not normally inspire a life aquatic but that is what had occurred. In the instant that the metal connected with his head with a resonant twang she had understood what had been wrong with the picture. Existence, her existence, in the car, in the supermarket, in traditional salsa lessons, in bed with M, with every costly breath taken, was drowning her.

She had driven to the sea a week later – to the sea at night, with its blueblack roar and lumbering grace. She had taken her shoes and socks off and stood in the October tide, her toes thrilled and frozen and looked out at its impossible shape with blind eyes. The sea could not parallel park, the sea did not eat five dinners every night, nor did it mock her poor dress sense. But the sea could be, was, magnificent, it took her breath away with every salt-filled swathe and in that moment, for her, she knew it was more of a husband to her than M could ever be.

CHAPTER 8

Along with a tendency towards the occasional homicide, the coupling of awe-inspiringly unstable individuals was another popular feature of M's family. On the night that Jonah, Daniel's grandfather, married Bernice, after the reception had ended (and the kerfuffle caused when Jonah had murdered his best man with a Corby Trouser Press had died down) but before the light switch of reality was flicked on again, they agreed to make lists of 'what if names' – names of people who burned so brightly that if you met them, your world would be shaken like a snow globe and for ever more disturbed. For Jonah, these people, glimpsed on a cinema screen as a child and thereafter craved like an addict yearning to recreate their first high, were intangible and magnificently obtrusive. For Bernice, the list was like the contents of a tidal pool, perfect until touched and then glacial and distorted.

Bernice's list was forgotten in a fold of her wedding dress, to be rediscovered a dozen years later when the fighting became so intense that a squall blew it from its hangar in the wardrobe where such sacred artefacts resided. They read it together sitting on the bedroom floor and it was restorative, so much so that they glimpsed the love that had entwined them on their wedding day, but they could not touch it.

There was a restaurant in London, a spectacularly exclusive restaurant, where people went to be seen and heard but not to eat. As a consequence, the owners of the restaurant had decided that there was no need to actually serve food. Food would be ordered, glorious food of unimaginable complexity and ingenuity, and empty plates would arrive and leave. This was a secret of the rich. It was impossible to book a table in such a restaurant but Jonah had called in a favour that had been bequeathed to him in his father's will. He was making an effort for their anniversary, in order to prove that he was the kind of man that he and Bernice knew he could never be (had never been).

In the restaurant, seated, they stared at each other in silence across an acre of pristine tableware, whilst the empty platitudes that filled the room to bursting point circled around Bernice's head and burrowed behind her eyes where they shrivelled and died. She rose from the table wordlessly in a quest for the toilet and almost immediately collided with a man of athletic build and an abundance of complicated facial features, redolent with celebrity iconography. He nodded a head adorned with a mantle of perfect greying curls in apology and followed her.

When Bernice returned she was unable to catch her breath. Jonah stared for a minute, something about her had changed inextricably. 'That man who collided with you, wasn't he…' Jonah left his words twisting in the conceptual breeze.

'Adam West,' Bernice replied. Her eyes scouted the room but there was nowhere to take cover in any direction.

'Your dress is inside out,' said Jonah, mainly with his hands. He was becoming animated. That was the way it always began.

'I saw you follow him into the men's toilet and he's on your list.' He was shaking now, his eyes blinking in the glare of her betrayal. 'Did you fuck him? On our anniversary?'

'It isn't that kind of list,' replied Bernice, playing with her cutlery, trying to disengage from the evening.

Jonah pushed his chair back from the table. This was escalating. He had no reverse gear.

'If you didn't fuck him, then what did you do with him, Bernice? What did you do that meant you had to get out of your dress and back into your dress in a men's toilet, I'm all ears?'

'I killed him,' muttered Bernice. 'I killed him and because of all the blood and there really was a great deal of blood, more than you could imagine, I washed my dress and turned it inside out so you wouldn't notice, but you did notice so that didn't work. Can we get the bill please?'

'You killed Batman.'

'I killed Batman.'

'Where is he now?' hissed Jonah.

'In one of the toilet stalls, well that's not quite true, his torso is in one of the toilet stalls, his head is in one of the cisterns. I suppose I panicked a little.'

Jonah sat back in his chair. The sheer enormity of scale of their current situation was one which life up to that point had left him somewhat ill equipped to cope with.

'You decapitated Batman,' Jonah whispered, shooting a glance at the direction of the last resting place of the caped crusader. 'Why?'

'Well, it's like you said,' replied Bernice calmly, smoothing down her dress. 'He was on my list.'

CHAPTER 9

M's memories of his life with Saul and his wife suggested that he lived a very different version of reality to the other participants.

'You appear to be living a very different version of reality to the other participants,' said M's wife (who was in the process of manufacturing Daniel in her womb), as she navigated Saul's buggy around the fronds of early morning frost that decorated the fringes of the paving slabs in Camden Market.

M bent down to pick up Saul's favourite toy 'face-face' which was a cross between a giraffe and a turtle and placed it back into his son's hand. M noticed that each tiny cuticle bore a mark which resembled the heliosphere of a diffused supernova. His son's smile was untainted by human frailty but more importantly there was no sign that he had inherited the affliction of unbridled rage.

M's wife brushed an illusory crumb from the lapel of her coat for the three hundredth time since leaving home that morning, clenched and unclenched her hands and tried to bring the world back into focus. Every item of her clothing was an identical shade of crimson but to her, her clothes were glaringly unmatched to a degree which made her feel nauseous whenever she caught sight of her reflection.

Saul threw face-face on the floor again where it garnered several muddy leaves.

'He keeps doing that,' she said without opening her teeth.

M picked the toy up again, flicked the leaves off and handed it back to Saul. He ran his fingers through his son's hair and he remembered the way that Saul had ensnared his heart when he was placed into his arms, seconds after he had been born. He would have been handed to his mother but she was being restrained by three hospital orderlies, having chinned her midwife with a flawless right hook when she had demanded that she 'push' one time too often.

'He likes the game,' said M.

'He likes irritating the fuck out of his mother. Did you know there are 2.2 million germs living on the average leaf?'

'No but I'm sure our two-year-old son does. He learned about biomechanical diversity right after singing baa baa black sheep whilst sitting in a nappy full of his own shite.'

Saul waved face-face in the air above his head, giggled and threw it towards the ground where it was caught in mid-air.

'I think this belongs to the little girl,' said a man whose expression was as resolutely desolate as a child's mitten abandoned in a field.

'Boy,' replied M.

'I see,' said the man, his tone laden with sarcasm. He knelt down and reached out a sullied hand towards Saul's pram which was swiftly intercepted by M's wife's stockinged calf.

'Trying to give the little girl back her toy,' said the man.

'Not going to happen,' said M's wife, snatching face-face from the man's grip by the ends of her fingertips and wondering whether Camden Markets Authority offered a quarantine facility to members of the public.

'No need to be like that,' said the man, raising himself to his full height like a giant smudge on a fading film poster.

'Cunt off and die, wank sack,' said M's wife with a high degree of proficiency.

A Magellanic cloud passed across the man's expression. He glanced at M who at this point in time (before Saul's death), weighed little more than a damp spaniel and fixed upon M's wife. He reached into the inside of his orange Puffa jacket and pointed a convincingly long kitchen knife in the direction of Saul's face.

'Give me your purse or I will stick the little girl, bitch.'

M observed the scene as if it was a cartoon strip. He watched a speech bubble emerge from his mouth and float above his head and in it were written the words 'put the knife down, I am a policeman'.

The man punched M in the face, the ring on his finger unzipped M's eyebrow and left it flapping like an errant caterpillar.

'If you say another word, I swear I will cut you so badly that the little girl won't be able to recognise you, now tell your slag to give me her purse before I stab up the child.'

Saul began to cry and reached out his arms for his mother and father. M's wife leant towards him and the man pushed her hard in the chest, causing her to fall backwards into an icy puddle.

M was familiar with the concept of rage. Given that his father had killed the best man at his own wedding with a Corby Trouser Press for forgetting the ring, and his mother had disembowelled a member of the crew of the *Starship Enterprise* before her twentieth birthday, it would be fair to say that he was aware that he may have inherited something of a short temper but thought he had always managed to keep it under check. He was determined to break the cycle and knew that if Saul glimpsed the darkness in his heart for even a second, it would spread like a virus to his son and to the generations to come. This little boy, this perfect little person was still a blank canvas. He knew every day as their eyes met that Saul was drinking in his father's persona, that every mannerism, every gesture was germinating the tiny shoots that would grow tall and proud into the man he would become. To uncork the bottle for even a moment would be a betrayal of the father M was determined to be. But M knew, as he felt his son's eyes fall upon him, that occasionally one has to make a tiny exception and cause really fucking severe physical damage to another person's body.

'I am really sorry,' said M, more to his son than the man whose leg he had just kicked so hard that the kneecap had spun around 360 degrees. As the man turned towards M with his knife, M's wife stood up and headbutted him. She noticed that the blood splattered from his ruined nose was almost imperceptible on her crimson jacket.

'Daddy is just going to take this man for a little walk,' said M's wife.

M picked the man up in a fireman's lift and dumped him onto a stall selling tiny opaque jars of artisan preserves, which were thrown scuttling across the Camden Town cobblestones in a thousand directions.

Saul had stopped crying but this expression was far worse. He looked calm, as if what he had witnessed was normal. M swore to himself that he would teach his son the vocabulary of patience and forgiveness but it was a language that M simply did not speak and had he tried, no one would have listened.

CHAPTER 10

Hampstead Police Station

July 23rd

Police interview with Mrs M.

Recording re-commences.

14.26 Detective Sergeant Ulstram enters the interview room to join Detective Sergeant Arnold.

DSU: Mrs M, I have heard your account of the events of the 16th July but would like to go over it one more time.

DSA: For the benefit of the recording, Mrs M shrugs her shoulders.

DSU: Can you explain why it was you travelled to Sainsburys supermarket in Swanage to do your shopping when it was 138 miles from your home in Kentish Town?

MM: They sold macaroons. Sainsburys in Kentish Town had run out.

DSU: You drove 138 miles for macaroons?

MM: I like macaroons.

DSU: And there was nowhere closer?

MM: That's exactly what my husband asked at the time, which is why I chose Swanage.

DSU: In order to be facetious?

MM: I wanted to see how far I could test his patience before he snapped.

DSU: And how far was it?

MM: On the North Circular, just after joining a line of stationary traffic on Hanger Lane – that's when he first tried to get out of the car. I didn't want him to get out of the car, so I kicked the central locking button so hard that it disappeared into the engine cavity. That pretty much meant he was never going to be able to get out of the car again. It all went downhill quite quickly from there.

DSU: Please deal with the confrontation with Mr Masumba.

MM: I had just parked up outside Sainsburys in Swanage, climbed out of the car window and got on to the car roof with a spade. Nothing particularly out of the ordinary. This parking attendant told me I couldn't stop my car diagonally across the entrance to the car park and I told him I obviously could because that's exactly what I had just done. I told him if he didn't like it he should get on to the car roof and tell me he didn't like it to my face.

DSU: And what happened?

MM: He got onto the car roof and told me he didn't like it to my face.

DSA: I'm sorry, where did you find a spade?

MM: In the boot of the car – Mr M always has a spade in the boot in case he needs it – he has never really explained why and it's not the kind of thing you ask Mr M about.

DSU: And where was Mr M during all this?

MM: He was still in the car – you've seen the size of him – he isn't climbing out of a car window any time soon.

DSU: So Mr Masumba and you were on the car roof.

MM: Yes, and I told him, sometimes you get a feeling inside you and it just grows and grows until it's burning your throat and screaming into every facet of your existence to get out and it becomes so big that all that is left of you is that feeling, but it makes you afraid because you know it is too big and if you let it out there will be nothing left of you. It is horror and it is hope and it is everything that identifies you and everything that wants to destroy you. It is every mountain and every climber and every avalanche all at once. So I told him to let me be on that car roof because that was all that there was of me.

DSU: And did Mr Masumba understand?

MM: No, he didn't, so I twatted him in the head with the spade and he fell off the car roof. He didn't say very much after that.

DSU: Didn't your husband try to intervene?

MM: He did try to slide over into the driver's seat, presumably to drive off with me on the roof but at thirty-two stone, that arse hasn't seen much sliding action over the past few years.

DSU: So Mr Masumba was lying on the ground and your husband was stuck in the car.

MM: And I stayed sitting on the car roof until someone came, which didn't take long, what with Mr Masumba screaming and the continual sound of the car horn, caused by my husband's left arse cheek having been wedged against it.

DSU: Can you explain why you hit Mr Masumba? It seems to have been very much out of character.

MM: I was angry, angrier than I have ever been in my life. It was nothing to do with the parking issue really, just what my husband had said to me a few minutes before.

DSU: Which was?

MM: Which was that I had killed our little boy, our first son, well, more that he told me that if it wasn't for me, he would still be alive. Which wasn't true. Well, maybe it was true but I had never allowed myself to think that way before and once I did, after he had opened the bottle and let out that genie I could never, have never been able to stop thinking it.

DSU: Your youngest son was killed in a car accident?

MM: Yes, he was only two, nearly three but never quite three. I was on my way to hospital to have Daniel and I was late, I'm always late, The Late Mrs M they call me. My husband was already at the hospital and I dithered and went back to check that the house was locked and the gas was off and the dog was locked in the back garden, except we didn't have a dog, he died the year before, my fault as well. But that's another one of my issues, this checking thing and if we had just left thirty seconds earlier perhaps I wouldn't have been in so much pain from the birth and…

DSU: But it wasn't your fault.

MM: There are a thousand degrees of fault, Detective Sergeant and one less would have kept my little boy alive. I know I made my husband angry, very angry, but what he said to me could never be unsaid, I could never be un-blamed and there we sat, Mr Masumba on the ground, me on the roof of the car and my husband, arse wedged on the horn of a car he never wanted, all of us hating each other more with every breath we took. He stole everything from me with those words, he stole my family and he stole my life and in that moment I knew that all I had left was the sea.

DSU: Mrs M standing up and removing her microphone. Mrs M, would you please sit down, Mrs M walking towards the interview room door and – she has collapsed, Mike, get her into the recovery position, interview ends at 2.42pm

CHAPTER 11

The adults in Daniel's life – the largely absent manic mermaid and the murderous blubber fest who were masquerading as parents – had long since abandoned any pretence of engaging with him positively. His existence merely added volume to their rabid disputes, fuel to the raging forest fire of their mutual contempt. It was therefore somewhat unfortunate that the remainder of Daniel's extravagantly dismal existence was dominated by Dorsal Grellman.

Dorsal Grellman was not a conventional school bully. His proficiency, his sheer despicable aplomb, was such that he commanded gratitude from those whose lives he systematically decimated. Dorsal was a pestilence, he inflicted himself on others, was wistfully destructive, impressionistic in his awful creativity. He was familiar with remorse as an abstract concept, just not one he had ever experienced. Teachers, rules, pain thresholds, laws, were irritating obstructions to be traversed. He had developed a second sense, a bat-like radar for victims and a hunger for their ruination which grew wilder with every taste.

Those who encountered Dorsal Grellman fleetingly as he unleashed his peculiar cruelty upon them might reasonably have assumed that he had been born in ancient Sparta, abandoned on a mountainside to perish, only to be discovered and raised by a pack of wolves. It was impossible to imagine that this determinedly poisonous, emotionally feral bastard had been the progeny of socially mobile and respectable parents who once loved and cherished him, as opposed to wild beasts who feasted upon the steaming innards of their victims.

There is an ill-conceived assumption that only an upbringing redolent with abuse could create a Dorsal Grellman. It isn't always violence which begets violence – in Dorsal's case it was the withdrawal of love which had hitherto been unconditional. He was not to know that there was a 'best before' date stamped on his parent's affections, an expiry date on their investment when they would withdraw all and leave him emotionally bankrupt.

A professional couple who cared perhaps a little too much for the facade of normality, Jester and Bethany Grellman built a pack of cards to reside in and placed baby Dorsal on the top floor. Jester was a futures broker doomed to constantly explain what he did to people who only heard the words 'die, die, die' when they looked at his large round face. Bethany fashioned intricate jewellery from the bleached ligaments and skulls of rodents which she sold from a market stall in Bermondsey. These weren't real jobs, but they were a symptom of the world we have created and there was no will to discover a cure. Dorsal was permanently embraced, stowed in a papoose on his father's back, wallowing in the shallow of his mother's arms, he was their tiny vision.

It was with a sense of unaccustomed clarity that one evening, over a glass of Chianti and some bratwurst, the Grellmans realised that their love for each other had been lost in the space between their own vacuous words. When the polarity was reversed in their marriage from attract to repel, the vortex created by the beating of their tiny insectile wings disappeared and there was nothing to prevent Dorsal from falling. He was falling still.

Dorsal's arms were outstretched but to his parents he had become a hazard to be navigated around. He learned that there was a poverty in love and a purity in hatred, that if he was to survive he must climb onto the shoulders of his victims to avoid becoming one himself. He had been placed in his aunt's home for a month whilst his parents 'found their feet' and the month never came to an end. He had become an invisible giant with eyes that would never forgive and his parents quickly filed him under 'exson'.

*

It was an autumnal Friday morning like any other. A starling opened the ailerons at the end of it's wings and described a perfect parabola as it swooped down to catch a worm; a squirrel secreted a hazelnut in a flowerbed, stopped to smell its own arse, forgot where the hazelnut was, turned back to try to find it, froze because it mistook a nearby dog turd for a fox, smelt its arse again, tried to bury the hazelnut it no longer had, found the original hazelnut, ate it, smelt its arse again, patted down the area where the hazelnut had been and left, pleased with a job well done. At the same time, Dorsal Grellman aged five, sat between his parents, inside the headmaster's study in the D'Oily Cart Academy waiting to be sold into slavery.

Caldwell Bynes swept past into his office, his unnecessarily swooshy cape following behind him, grasped with flailing desperation by his redoubtable secretary Bennett as if she were the bridesmaid and the bride's trailing gown was an unexploded World War 2 bomb coated in butter.

'So how exactly does this work?' asked Dorsal's father, granting the conversation exactly sixty per cent of his attention whilst dividing up the balance between thinking about what to buy his girlfriend for her nineteenth birthday, whether or not they should eat at the Italian restaurant in the Fulham Road again and how he should say goodbye to his son when he had no intention of ever visiting him.

'We will visit you of course,' added his father, squeezing his son's limp hand and messing his lank, unmanageable hair.

'You sign here,' said Caldwell, pushing a long, handwritten parchment across his unnecessarily sumptuous desk with the tip of his be-ringed little finger, causing a scraping sound akin to the death throes of a scarab beetle.

'Is this even legal?' asked Dorsal's mother, somewhat belatedly, her flawless lipstick glinting in the same fulsome sunbeams that caused the tears on her son's cheeks to glisten like uncut diamonds as they clung to his chin.

'Legal?' said Caldwell Bynes. 'Fuck me no. Not even slightly. Any other questions, because I have a school to run and other parents to…'

'What will he have to, well, you know, do?' asked his mother.

'Do?' asked Caldwell Bynes. 'If you are looking to me to assuage any guilt which might still be lurking in the far reaches of your consciences then you have come to the wrong place. He will have three square meals a day, he will have his own cell in the school dungeon which he can decorate as he pleases and he will be trained by some of the finest bullies this country has ever produced. He will be required to behave in an unreasonable and excessively punitive manner towards the pupils and staff of the school alike and when he reaches the age of eighteen he will be set free to practise the skills he has learned on an unsuspecting society.'

'Have you any advice for us?' asked Dorsal's father.

'Well, you might want to think about, you know, hiding.'

'Why would we need to do that?' asked Dorsal's mother uneasily.

'Revenge,' replied Caldwell Bynes. 'Our official school bullies do have a bit of a habit of hunting down their parents after they have been released from a life of misery and servitude and sort of, you know, executing them.

Nothing at all to worry about, just make sure you change your identities and leave the country. A bit of plastic surgery wouldn't do any harm.'

As they stood to go, Dorsal's parents turned to look at their son, to really look at him for the first time since they had begun their new lives in which he played no part. The tears had stopped falling, leaving room on his face for something else. It was not something that either of them had seen on the face of a child before and for the first time since they had grown to abhor each other they instinctively reached out and held hands.

*

Some three years later, when Daniel M first walked in through Dorsal Grellman's school gate – for, through his love of the enterprise of school, Dorsal had become proprietorial, even jealous of this chocolate box of torture – he could not at first take in what he was seeing. This termite, in full school uniform, with a life vest strapped to its back, was the person-ification of defeat; his destruction would be an almost victimless crime. Dorsal sighed. Daniel did not merit the premiership-quality beating he was about to receive, but it was Dorsal's duty to inflict it upon him all the same.

Daniel picked through the detritus of the schoolyard – a nondescript condominium of mouldering vomit-coloured cubes, a dusting of random children toiling away at the act of being and in the middle of this picture and looming ever larger what appeared to be a brick wall. The brick wall was wearing a school tie and jacket and there was something strangely familiar about it – it was the eyes that teetered in a perfectly square brick head, they reminded Daniel of his father's eyes, perhaps not in appearance but in intent. They wanted to kill him.

'What are you?' asked the giant of a boy who stood not just in front of him, but all around him. He blocked out the sun. He was the rain. Daniel had never been asked what he was before, and he pondered the question for a moment, sensing that his answer was extremely important.

It wasn't.

'I'm...' started Daniel.

This was quite enough for Dorsal.

The punch was delivered with animalistic precision and viscosity of movement. To Daniel it felt like a 1972 Vauxhall Viva with all-leather inte-rior and walnut dashboard had fallen off the roof of a car park directly onto his head. His shoes were dispatched to opposite ends of the playground, his right trouser leg was separated from the left so comprehensively that it was never found again and his pants were turned inside out.

His work done, Dorsal departed.

Daniel tried to reassemble himself but he had literally been disembodied. He sensed more than saw that he was not alone in the uneven patch of mossy concrete he currently occupied; there was another schoolboy staring down at him. He appeared to be wearing two pairs of glasses and inhabited a body shaped like a walnut. Daniel was not entirely certain that this was not actually a walnut.

'The force is strong in that one,' said the boy, which was the kind of comment that made people want to kick him into the air so hard that he never came down again.

He proffered a helping hand, causing his sleeve to ride up exposing three watches. Finally Daniel was able to focus on the boy's face – he was indeed wearing two pairs of glasses and an expression which suggested that he was not well accustomed to being liked.

'My name's Ferris,' he said, and sadly for Ferris, it was.

'Daniel M,' said Daniel, who felt like he was standing and falling over all at the same time.

Ferris threw his pustulant arms around Daniel. 'Are we friends now? Yes, I think we are friends. That means we can do everything together – Science Club and Film Club and Tree Club, well, there isn't a Tree Club yet but we could start one and you could come to my home and watch me play with my Star Wars toys – you can't touch them obviously – and you can learn to play Dungeons and Dragons, I am a very powerful warlord and you can be my slave and carry my armour and we can swap clothes and pretend to be each other in lessons and…' Ferris was perspiring heavily and his head was bright red, it looked as if it might just implode.

Daniel looked at Ferris, at the rabid edifice of the school and back at Ferris. He began to yearn for the simplicity of being punched in the face.

*

When Daniel returned home from school that evening, M did not look at Daniel, or what was left of Daniel after the beating meted out by Dorsal, but at his life vest.

'We are going mountain climbing this weekend and you are going to thoroughly enjoy it,' said M. 'We haven't done anything together since you had all that fun in the dinghy.'

'Fun?' asked Daniel, quizzically.

'You can bring your life vest,' said M.

It occurred to Daniel that a life vest would be divested of many of its essential lifesaving qualities halfway up a mountain. Some might actually consider it a dangerous encumbrance.

CHAPTER 12

It was not the slap on the arse from the midwife that made baby Caldwell Bynes scream but the realisation that life had been inflicted upon him without his consent and could only, at its very best, be endured.

An execrable childhood which he traversed as gracelessly as a one-legged turkey on a treadmill left Caldwell ill-prepared for the lonely travails of adult existence. Below the palisades which barely contained his virulent self-loathing lay the verdant fields in which he cultivated the true focus of his contempt for the human race – children. They were the flag bearers for the void in his life that he could never fill and as such, they had become the enemy. How unfortunate it was then for all concerned, that Caldwell should arrive at the end of a road of diverse career paths, which included bovine proctology, cat de-clawing and chemical deforestation, as head teacher of the largest and almost certainly the worst comprehensive school in North London.

The D'Oily Cart Academy (or The Cart as it was known locally) scored so badly in the league table created by the Department for Education to measure academic achievement that they had to re-define the concept of failure. The only reason it was not closed after Caldwell's first Ofsted assessment was the fear for the unsuspecting national education system upon which the massed hordes of the unwashed within would be unleashed. It became, thereafter, the scholastic equivalent of Hadrian's Wall.

Caldwell stared at his desk, an unloved carbuncle encrusted with the offal of a thousand microwaved lunches, and then at his at his hands which lay before him like dead weights. His fingers, long and slender but inelegant, crawled outwards like giant elongated maggots.

A red light was flashing on what remained of his telephone. Having been smashed into submission with its handset repeatedly, it was functional only as a reflection of Caldwell's own state of decrepitude and to indicate that his secretary, Bennett, who, like the telephone, maintained a dogged unwillingness to die, wanted to communicate with him.

Bennett surfaced from her office that had once been a toilet cubicle, opened the door to the head teacher's study imperceptibly, in anticipation of a barrage of abuse, and searched for the least provocative way to deliver what would be monumentally unwelcome news.

'Head teacher, you have a child to see you.'

Caldwell retreated briefly from his vale of tears and formed his mouth into a single syllable.

'M?'

'Yes, head teacher.'

So it was Daniel M again.

In the endless minutes of silence that followed, Bennett ushered Daniel, life vest and all, into the study. There was an empty chair opposite the headmaster's desk but it was clearly not intended for sitting, so Daniel stood, legs all but buckling under the weight that lay upon his tiny shoulders.

'My father is planning to kill me this weekend, head teacher.'

'Again?'

'Yes, head teacher, again.'

'And yet you appear to be persistently alive, Daniel M.' He pronounced Daniel's surname as if exhaling a cough sweet that had been lodged deep in his oesophagus.

'Aren't you supposed to do something about this sort of thing? What happens if one day he actually succeeds in killing me?' asked Daniel.

'Do let me know if that happens.'

Daniel searched the head teacher's mucus-laden eyes for a sign that empathy might once at least have passed them by. He emerged empty-handed.

'Dorsal Grellman is trying to decapitate me.'

'I should hope so, it's his job,' replied Bynes.

'His job?'

'I am sorry, no, perhaps not his job, that is somewhat simplistic – it is his role.'

'His role is to try to decapitate me?' asked Daniel

'His role is to build your character, yours is to have your character built – if he actually manages to decapitate you in the process then that is unfortunate, but I am sure that you would agree it is a necessary part of growing up.'

Daniel had only one more card to play. His lips wavered; it certainly could not be characterised as an ace.

'My grandmother killed Batman.'

Caldwell stared at Daniel and then beyond him, far, far beyond him, into a future glutted with nothing but pain.

'Have your parents ever explained to you what you are?'

That question again.

'You are a rabbit in the crosshairs, Daniel M, an atrocity in waiting, you are every victim and everything that is not you is your predator. So you had better learn to run and you had better learn to hide and now you had better learn to leave.'

Daniel wanted to ask his head teacher, if not to advise, then at least to expand, but Caldwell was once again engrossed with his hands, each line a furrow ploughed with barren seed, at each intersection a poisoned well. The conversation, if that is what it had been, was at an end.

CHAPTER 13

The expressions on the faces of the Kentish Town girls' Under 9s swimming team were a complex combination of fear, anguish, disbelief and fear (again). Elissa Wage, their coach, followed their tiny pinched mouths from left to right and back again until they became a single Munch-like scream.

The woman, dressed in a tattered red one-piece swimming costume decorated with smiley faces, sat on the edge of a wooden bench, her wrecked hands covering her face, her body quaking as if she was receiving electro convulsive therapy. The changing room reverberated with the sound of silent tears crashing through grasping fingers on to tiled flooring and calloused toes. Elissa could see bloody fingerprints covering the half open locker above the woman's head and on the upper parts of her naked arms as if she had, at one point, embraced herself. Turning to find the entire Under 9s class standing en masse behind her, she wordlessly gathered them into a bouquet and ushered them to the far side of the changing room.

Returning, Elissa reached out a hand but then withdrew it; there was no part of this woman she could touch which would not somehow infringe her wordless rapture. A vocabulary limited in the main to aquatic terminology left Elissa at an immediate disadvantage when it came to assuaging this level of distress. She tried, 'Can I help?' Although she believed herself to be at least three hundred lengths of standard breaststroke away from being able to do so.

'I am here for the 9am adults' beginner's class,' the woman replied, through grey-blue fingers which masked her face like bloodied vine leaves.

'Well, it's 3pm now so you've missed it.'

'I know I've missed it. I was here on time but then I wasn't sure if I'd left my purse in the locker, so I opened the locker to look and there it was. So I closed the locker and then I thought, what if all my credit cards have expired, so I opened the locker and checked. Then I heard my mobile phone go off, so I had to go back to open the locker and check but then I remembered I don't have a mobile phone. But when I looked in the locker again I remembered our dog and my son, sorry, my ex-son and ex-dog and the parking attendant and the police and I had a little cry. So then it occurred to me – what if I go swimming and my locker key falls off into the water and because I can't swim, I can't get it back and then I can't open my locker so I would have no money and no clothes. So I put my locker key into my locker so I wouldn't lose it. But then my locker key was locked in my locker. So then I didn't have my locker key or my clothes or my credit cards because they were all in my locker and I thought – I'm fucked. So I had to get them all back. But these modern lockers are really difficult to open, I had to get my fingers into this little gap that isn't big enough for fingers and it really, really hurt and at least two of my nails were just torn off – right off, but in the end I did it. Then I had my key back but of course no locker and no fingers – they were both kind of ruined.'

The woman looked up at Elissa with eyes that had endured so much wretched honesty that they had become dispossessed. They were the eyes of the drowned.

'Why don't you have a cup of tea in my office and when I'm finished with the girls I'll give you a swimming lesson on the house?' suggested Elissa.

The woman rose almost balletically and then sat down heavily as if punched in the solar plexus. She recognised the distant glint of generosity but had no means of reaching it.

'What about all this?' her expansive gesture appeared to include the entirety of human existence, which was slightly beyond Elissa's brief.

'I can give you a swimming lesson and we can keep your things in my office, which I will lock,' Elissa replied. 'I can't help with all the rest.'

'What if you forget?'

'Forget?'

'Forget to lock the office or lose your key.'

'I won't.' Elissa proffered her hand and the woman snatched it greedily as if she intended to keep it.

'You might forget me.'

'I won't.' She held the woman's hand in both of hers.

But Daniel's mother knew she would. She had become bereft – a mother without her children, a wife in a fictional marriage and now a mermaid who couldn't swim.

*

Jonah's telephone dragged him roughly from the brink of sleep. He stared at the caller display and contemplated evasion but Bernice had already discovered all his hiding places.

'Where are you?' he asked.

'I'm where you left me.'

'I left you on the edge of a cliff and told you to jump.'

'Well I didn't like that advice,' said Bernice.

'But that was yesterday, surely…'

'Obviously I haven't been there ever since. I have to talk to you about the list.'

'The fucking list. I destroyed the fucking list, I rammed it down the toilet and then I rammed your head down after it.'

'That didn't work, I'm afraid, apart from making me permanently deaf in one ear and making me want to vomit when I hear your voice, it didn't work.'

'What do you want me to do?' asked Jonah.

'I want you to save the one man left on the list. I want you to get in my way and I want you to stop me doing this a third time.'

'Don't you mean a second time?'

There was a muffled incoherent noise, like the mewling of a poisoned rat before it dies.

''fraid not.'

The noise became louder, imploring. Bernice grunted with effort as if shoving a huge weight away from her towards the edge of the cliff and then there was nothing.

'So,' she resumed, breathlessly, 'will you stop me?'

'What have you done?' But he knew all too well what she had done.

She had just pushed Darth Vader off Beachy Head.

CHAPTER 14

Saturday had arrived as Saturdays do and Daniel had woken at 4am to find his father standing over his bed, sharpening a meat cleaver and singing the aria 'One Fine Day' from Puccini's *Madame Butterfly*. Nothing out of the ordinary there then.

'Up we get,' said M, whipping off his duvet with the speed and dexterity of a thirty-two stone bullfighter and leading Daniel out of his bedroom by his wrist. He had never held Daniel by his hand. Holding Daniel's hand would have promised a degree of intimacy that his father had no facility to deliver – that particular cupboard was bare.

'Shall I get dressed, Dad?' asked Daniel as M dragged him down the stairs of their house towards the front door, 'because I'm only in my pyjamas and it's quite cold.' M paused and looked down at him. His eyes seemed to soften for a moment. 'I never wanted this, but this is all we have left, you and I. It's what we are.' In that moment, the calm waters which still filled some of the tidal pools in M's heart were finally swept away and the bitter current that carried them left no way for them to return.

'What is the meat cleaver for, Dad?' asked Daniel, already aware that this was a question to which he did not want a response. But he had come to realise that no matter how bad answers might be, surprises were far, far worse.

'For little fingers and CCTV cameras,' replied M, looking at him as if this had been obvious. In many ways, it had been.

*

'This is the mountain that you will be climbing,' said M gesturing towards nothing that was remotely mountain-like as far as Daniel could see but plenty of things that had the potential to cause him irreparable harm.

M had driven them to St Pancras station and had parked just outside the multi-storey car park. Realisation dawned upon Daniel in the manner of a veal calf, exposed to light for the first time, only to discover it was the neon glare of the slaughterhouse.

The Austin Allegro struggled up the ramps of the car park to the top level, encumbered by the combined weight of expectation and M's arse. After disengaging said arse from the long suffering driver's seat, M waddled over to the nearest CCTV camera, hacked it from the wall with a single blow of the meat cleaver and crushed it underfoot as if it were a fag butt. He was looking at Daniel's life vest with unaccustomed satisfaction. It occurred to Daniel that his father was much more interested in the falling aspects of climbing than the ascending parts.

At the edge of the car park balustrade, Daniel and his father paused and wordlessly shared a glance over the top into the abyss.

'Off you pop then, Daniel,' said M, gesturing vaguely towards the wide blue yonder, 'show me what you're made of.'

'What if I get to the bottom, Dad, can we go home?'

There was a further period of silence whilst Daniel and M looked over the balustrade, their eyes following each of the six floors of sheer concrete, down to the frost-licked pavement far below where a cat had paused to probe an errant ear. It looked like a furry ant. There were indents in the surface of the concrete but they were no more substantial than a day's growth of stubble. Spiderman would have struggled with this task, little boys in pyjamas weighed down by life vests had no need to apply.

Daniel looked back at his father – his question was redundant. From the impatient manner in which M was tapping the meat cleaver against his thigh he did not think he had time to launch an expedition to locate his father's better nature.

So this was fear.

Daniel climbed on to the edge of the balustrade and lowered himself onto the first of the more prominent bricks. His fingers and toes were small enough to gain some purchase and with desperate precision he edged down inch by inch.

After two minutes he had actually begun to believe that he might make it all the way but without warning he lost his grip and began to slip and then fall backwards. With every sinew in his body he tried to remain connected to the wall but soon his only foothold was in thin air which is, by and large, less substantial than concrete.

M saw his son begin to fall and a smile passed across his face like a newly dawned sun. He swirled the feeling of fulfilment around his mouth like a delicious Belgian chocolate but there was a lingering aftertaste of something unfamiliar – regret? His life was like an express train without a destination, a race horse with no finishing line. He had cradled his dead son in his arms and now he could not escape from death, it clogged his pores, impeded his every breath and his only choice was to deliver his burden to Daniel. So not regret, no, but also not resolution.

Daniel had stopped falling. Gravity's embrace was inexorable and yet he had defied it. The life vest had snagged on a light fixture, leaving Daniel suspended twenty metres from the pavement.

'Ohforfuckssake,' said M and not without due cause. He began to run towards his car but whilst his feet were willing, the ham hocks that now occupied the positions his ankles used to be in showed little inclination to follow suit. He turned back and leaned over to get a better look at what was holding the life vest in place but it was what he heard that persuaded him to head back to his car again. The life vest was ripping apart under Daniel's weight.

M reached the penultimate level of the car park to find his son just over an arm's length below him. Part of the life vest had been shredded and the part which remained attached to the light fitting would bear Daniel's weight for only a few seconds more. M found himself reaching out a hand as Daniel looked up and reached out his own. As they extended their reaches, their fingertips touched, before the life vest gave way and Daniel fell again, clawing for the hand of the man who had killed him.

Daniel's father looked beyond his extended grasp towards the area of pavement where his son would shortly explode only to see it filled by a milk float.

*

The milkman's usually unremarkable progress was impeded as a 1974 Austin Allegro screeched to a halt across his path. The entire car appeared to resonate as a behemoth struggled to escape from behind the steering wheel and gradually unfurled itself out of the driver's door.

The enormous unit that was Daniel's father walked directly up to the milk float and motioned a single meaty hand skywards.

'Couldn't lend me a hand, could you – there's a child on your roof that belongs to me?'

The milkman stepped up on his seat and peered onto the roof of the float where a boy in pyjamas was sitting. The boy waved at him apologetically. The milkman pulled away as if slapped in the face, checked the milk float roof again where the child was still waving, reached up, grabbed the child and handed him down to his father.

'Where…?' was the milkman's sole contribution.

'Fell off the car park, sleepwalking again, he's a bastard for it,' said Daniel's father as he deposited Daniel rather too vigorously into the passenger seat.

They were both shaking as the Austin Allegro threaded its way back through the ice kissed streets of North West London. Daniel looked at M's expressionless face, his eyes illuminated like tiny neon shop signs as he reached behind Daniel's seat and handed him a blanket. He glanced at Daniel and said, 'This changes nothing,' but the snow globe they occupied had just been shaken vigorously once again.

CHAPTER 15

It was the morning of the accident (again).

Daniel's mother lay in her tiny bed in her tiny bedsit, legs clasped to her chest in the best approximation of sleep that her brain would currently facilitate. The dream was set on loop, it had devoured her piece by piece until she had become unidentifiable. Sleep was nothing more than a conduit.

She was in the car on the way to the Royal Free hospital with Daniel performing a passable breaststroke in the amniotic fluid of her womb whilst Saul, then her only child, sat in the back seat singing to himself.

Daniel's mother experienced the world as if her eyes were covered by a veil woven from the silk of poisonous spiders. Written words fell from her ears like tiny font-shaped raindrops, traffic lights fired transparent lies into her hair which she could never wash out, zebra crossings were gateways to heaven and Hades. Some would have considered this a handicap to driving, but Daniel's mother had checked the Highway Code only that morning and since there was no mention of any of these hazards she considered that she was good to go.

Saul resided in the rear-view mirror and that was how she remembered him, in reverse, imprisoned in a letterbox of glass. His eyes fell on hers; it was all he could offer her from where he sat. They were the eyes of a child who is blind to the inadequacies of the human condition. Returning to the road, she saw too late that she had gone straight through a red light and a bus was bearing down on her like a slack-jawed lion, inches from its prey. She slammed her feet onto the brake and the accelerator at the same time and the Austin Allegro performed a vehicular pirouette, avoiding the bus by the width of a coat of paint and sailing through the intersection to the other side. And all the while, Saul's smiling eyes, oblivious and unquestioning, kissed hers, his voice adulterating a half-glimpsed nursery rhyme.

The car mounted the pavement, scattering a cluster of pedestrians like a pile of protesting autumn leaves caught by a sudden gust of wind. Daniel completed another length of breaststroke with a backflip and kicked out with both feet to launch himself forwards once again into the dark waters of their mutual DNA. She could see his heels push out of the fabric of her smock and gasped at the audacity of the pain. The cramps which had been staccato had now assumed the rapidity of machine gun fire.

'Saul.'

She turned around in her seat and reached out a hand for her little man. Sometimes she dreamt that she had held him, in those few moments, felt him breathe laughter onto her face, that she had warned him about the treachery of life, how to navigate the forests of carrots and sticks. But she could no more reach him now than she did then.

As the car careered inexorably onwards she touched her legs, warm and cold at the same time. Her waters had broken. She looked into the face of the traffic warden who was screaming at her through her driver's window, at the taxi driver, at the policeman. She was a goldfish and this was her bowl – she swam for their entertainment and within her Daniel swam no more.

She pulled into a line of slow moving traffic, hitting the rear bumper of a camper van and turned into the path of an oncoming motorcyclist who embraced the passenger side of her car and crumpled onto the unforgiving tarmac. She had to reach the hospital but she no longer knew what a hospital was, it was a word, a destination which was all around her. The contractions were unendurable, she was giving birth in the driver's seat of an Austin Allegro whilst driving at speed down the pavement of Haverstock Hill. Had it been 1965 she would have reached the Accident and Emergency Department of the Royal Free hospital with seconds to spare, but it was not 1965 and someone had put a supermarket in her way.

The Austin Allegro entered Budgens through the main window, ruining the two-for-one disinfectant display and continued through the fruit and vegetable aisle towards the delicatessen. Impeded by a tower-high display of Ferrero Rocher and the deputy supermarket manager who had climbed it shortly before, the car took out the National Lottery stand, and eventually came to a halt in the middle of a Star Wars promotion. It had stopped because Daniel's mother had finally applied the brakes and because the engine had fallen out when the car totalled R2-D2. When she looked down, she saw Daniel's head had begun to emerge from between her legs.

Saul had stopped singing.

It was not anticipated when the Star Wars advertising promotion was designed, that Luke Skywalker would be hit by an Austin Allegro travelling at forty miles per hour through the fruit and vegetable aisle of Budgens in Belsize Park. No consideration was given, therefore, to the possibility that the Jedi Knight's lightsabre would smash through the side window of a car and strike a child with such force that it would stop his heart.

There were so many people swimming in Daniel's mother's fishbowl now – she screamed until she thought her lungs would implode but she could not make a sound. Constrained by her seatbelt, shoulders dusted with broken glass and Saul, his first kiss, his wedding day when he could not stop laughing, his own children whose faces mirrored his sleeping sigh, smashed into tiny pieces.

The light had gone out behind his eyes and she could not remember how to turn it back on.

CHAPTER 16

If the quality of Daniel's schooling experience was somewhat diminished by the despicable cruelty of Dorsal Grellman, the official school bully, then the explosion of his chemistry teacher certainly did little to mitigate this.

Chemistry lessons in Daniel's year were defined by superlatives. The unboundaried abhorrence which his chemistry teacher, Mrs Ritz, felt for Daniel's only friend, Ferris, was surpassed only by Ferris' love of Mrs Ritz and all things Ritz-related.

On the first day of the school year, a sparkling new set of eight-year-olds had trooped into their first ever chemistry lesson. Brimming with early term exuberance, Mrs Ritz set the children what she thought would be a simple and exciting project which they would file away in their memories in the cabinet marked 'inspirational teacher.' They were to collect samples of everyday substances which they found in their home in a petri dish and these would be viewed under a microscope. The class would then write essays about what they had learnt.

Mrs Ritz sighed with self-approbation after she had given out the project sheets and carefully wrapped petri dishes. She could almost hear the whir of eager young minds. Oh, she was good at this.

A hand rose abruptly at the back of the class and begun rotating like an agitated windmill. The hand was attached to a diminutive child who appeared to be wearing two pairs of glasses and three watches and was beaming at her in a way she found disconcerting. The boy was sitting next to Daniel M, who appeared to be shrinking down under his desk.

'Yes...' she checked the register. 'Ferris.'

The bespectacled child was demonstrably excited to be spoken to with a tone of voice that was not contemptuous.

'We can take a sample of anything?' asked Ferris.

'Obviously ask your parents for their consent,' replied Mrs Ritz. She thought she had seen Ferris shudder when she said the word 'parents'. 'But yes, any everyday substance you like.'

'Anything?' repeated Ferris incredulously.

A frisson of discomfort burrowed down into the verdant soil which lightly covered the forest of Mrs Ritz's sanity and began to take root. There was something about this child that was discordant but what could an eight-year-old find at home given one evening that could be remotely problematic? She chuckled to herself, smoothed down the pleats of her best grey skirt and smiled.

'Anything at all, Ferris.'

*

The following morning 4c trooped into the classroom and as she had expected, their eyes were ablaze with barely restrained excitement. They carefully placed their petri dishes on the desks in front of them. Mrs Ritz had already set the microscope up so that the samples taken would be enlarged and projected on to a screen.

'Johnstone Fenner,' she shouted. A distended ginger face snapped to attention, regarded her earnestly and stood up with a sample which he described as 'dog bits'.

Each one of the slides was more mundane than the next but what should have been a joyous experience for Mrs Ritz was diminished by the feeling that Ferris' eyes were burrowing ever deeper into her spine. She walked over to his desk but his petri dish appeared to be pristine and empty.

'Why haven't you brought a sample, Ferris? Everyone else has.' She felt an inexplicable light snowfall of relief dust the cappuccino of her day.

Ferris looked wounded but quickly recovered. 'I have brought you a sample.'

Mrs Ritz snatched the dish and held it up to the light – quite empty.

'If this is a game, Ferris, then it is not amusing,' snapped Mrs Ritz. She tried to take the lid off the petri dish but it seemed stubbornly closed.

'It's not a game, Mrs Ritz,' replied Ferris, 'you said we should bring a sample from home and I have. It's bubonic plague. I probably wouldn't be opening it if I were you.'

'Of course it isn't bubonic plague, you stupid child.' She had tried to fit the edge of a biro into the side of the lid and it began to give a little. She looked at Ferris for a moment and was about to send him to the headmaster but there was a hue of honesty which emanated from his glowing rat-like features that gave her cause to feel slightly less sure of herself.

'How could you possibly have put bubonic plague into this petri dish?' Now the biro lid was wedged behind the lid and she pulled at it angrily.

'My dad – my dead dad – was a microbiologist for the Ministry of Defence and he used our garden shed as a laboratory. The big black lead-lined case said that this was bubonic plague but I suppose you might be – '

The lid popped open and a hundred billion tiny kisses exited the petri dish in search of a party.

*

The school had never had cause to call in a HazMat team before and it would be fair to say that the half mile cordon and enforced disinfection and hospitalisation of every child and teacher did reduce the popularity of their ordinarily well attended 'bring and buy' sale to an all time low.

Worst of all, Mrs Ritz was compelled to amend her hitherto pristine CV with the words 'an uninterrupted teaching career of twenty years during which I have achieved three national distinctions and almost no children have been infected with the black death'.

Ferris' subsequent essay titled 'How Small-minded Bureaucrat Obsession with Health and Safety is Shackling our Schools' was shredded in front of the entire assembly and Dorsal Grellman was permitted to dangle him from the picture window of the science block by his nose.

*

After what became known as 'the least successful chemistry project in the history of schooling,' Mrs Ritz and the headmaster agreed that giving Ferris an 'open brief' on such occasions had been decidedly ill-conceived. The school year progressed and Dorsal was allowed to perpetrate almost unendurable malfeasance upon staff and children alike on a daily basis. Ferris had begun following Mrs Ritz home and posting love letters through her front door but after her husband set their two attack Dobermanns on him, all was peaceful and as it should be. It was the kind of peace experienced, for example, just before a plasma storm engulfs and destroys mankind's biometrical system causing the decimation of the human race.

Over the months, Mrs Ritz had seen the ragtag group of random children in her chemistry class grow to become a slightly older ragtag group of random children. It was therefore with lowered defences that she set them a project for the spring holiday titled 'create a science experiment to demonstrate to the class' (to which was hurriedly added) 'not involving weapons grade biological components.'

Mrs Ritz was pleased to see the children return after the break laden with a treasure trove of uninspiring and tedious experiments such as 'does an orange sink or float', 'seed germination', 'stabbing a potato with a matchstick' and 'making a snowflake'.

Daniel and Ferris arrived slightly after Jeremy Frapper had demonstrated 'how to bend a straw' and they were carrying something large and rectangular cloaked by an old curtain. Mrs Ritz observed them with a degree of trepidation normally reserved for an Apollo pilot who has noticed that a piece of critically important spacecraft has dropped off just after leaving the orbit of the earth.

'What is this?' demanded Mrs Ritz.

'An old fish tank,' replied Ferris, pulling back the curtain to reveal an old fish tank.

'And why did you involve Daniel in this project, Ferris?'

'He had an old fish tank, Mrs Ritz,' replied Ferris.

'And that was his sole contribution to this project?' asked Mrs Ritz.

There was a moment of silence, something passed between Daniel and Ferris, a sense of recognition of a creative role that was beyond words, akin perhaps to that played by Covington for Darwin or Eddington for Einstein.

'I helped him carry the fish tank,' said Daniel.

'I see,' said Mrs Ritz, who did not see. 'And what exactly do you call this project Ferris, because to me it looks like a sort of…'

She looked more closely at the contents of the fish tank, at the device that was now flashing with purple and orange lights. It reminded her of photographs she had once seen of a laboratory in – where had it been…?

Chernobyl, recalled Mrs Ritz.

'Cold fusion,' said Ferris. 'I call it cold fusion.'

'Cold fusion,' said Mrs Ritz. A bead of sweat appeared from nowhere and dripped off the end of her chin. She peered through at the interior of the grubby fish tank once again. This had become more difficult because stress was causing her left eye to open and close randomly.

'A theoretical nuclear reaction that occurs at relatively low temperatures under certain specific laboratory conditions,' explained Ferris.

'Except of course it isn't theoretical any more because, well, because Ferris has made it happen,' added Daniel.

Mrs Ritz called upon all the child handling techniques learned in twenty long years at the coalface of lower league schooling. She knew exactly how to address this situation professionally and in a child-centred manner, which would meet the needs of the young person involved from both a teaching and an interpersonal perspective.

'Like fuck you have,' she said, shoving Ferris in the face, ripping the lid from the tank and grabbing hold of what seemed to be a dirty fish tank pump with some fairy lights strapped to it but was in fact the first low-temperature atomic deuterium reactor ever created by the human race.

Ferris pulled Daniel back behind him as soon as he saw what was about to happen which, given that he was only the size of an ample otter, afforded little protection.

To say Mrs Ritz was vaporised would be an over-simplification of what was a complex series of subatomic chemical reactions, all of which occurred within milliseconds. Safe to say that nothing remotely Mrs Ritz-like remained, other than her left ear lobe, which proved to be stubbornly indestructible and was therefore the subject of much excitement in the scientific community for many years to come.

Being coated with your chemistry teacher was not a moment which edified Daniel's scholastic experience but it did provide him with a sense that life was and would continue to be a meteor-storm for which he had no umbrella.

CHAPTER 17

It was the summer of 1964. Lyndon Johnson was in the White House, Elvis Presley's magnum opus *Kissin' Cousins* was packing out British cinemas, mankind was five years away from setting foot in the Sea of Tranquillity and Felicia Freeziwater was a liar.

Felicia's husband, Jaques, pushed his chair away from the dining table, took off his horn-rimmed bifocals, folded them with deliberate precision, put them into their red leatherette case, put the case on the smoked glass dining table, moved his dinner plate minutely in a clockwise direction, lit up a cigarette, inhaled languorously, exhaled with Shakespearean bravura, ran his fingers through his lustrous flaxen hair, moved his dinner plate minutely in an anticlockwise direction, put out the cigarette, interlaced his fingers, sighed and fixed his wife with the look of monumental disappointment normally reserved for a kitten which has just shat on your foot.

Felicia picked up his glasses case, walked over to the oven, opened the door, set the grill temperature to 250 degrees, put the glasses case into the oven, closed the door and returned to her seat.

'It isn't possible for a three-year-old child to do that,' squinted Jaques.

'It fucking well is and she fucking well did,' replied Felicia.

'Let's just say for a second she managed to work out how to break into our car, hot-wire it and get it started just like you say she did, how exactly do you suggest she managed to reach the foot pedals and steer it for three miles to the park? She's only two foot nine inches tall?'

Felicia peered over Jaques' shoulder to the crime against humanity which was their stainless steel framed, maroon, corduroy and pine settee where their daughter '!' nestled expressionlessly stroking their dog, Sir Laurence Olivier, a French bulldog, which she had dressed up like Queen Elizabeth the First.

'Don't look at me, I am so ashamed,' thought Sir Laurence Olivier.

'!' was putting the final bow into Sir Laurence Olivier's wig and was not listening to their conversation in a way which made it obvious that she was listening to their conversation.

'Why don't you ask your daughter, Felicia?' asked Jaques, once again demonstrating eloquently the reason why stepchildren experience child-hood on the margins of a family and sometimes drift off the page alto-gether.

'!', who was now not listening intently, began to paint Sir Laurence Olivier's claws cobalt blue.

Felicia pulled Jaques' tie out from his suit jacket, picked up a carving knife, hacked it off just below the knot, popped it on top of the bubbling cheese fondue, stirred it around carefully with a fondue fork, removed it and plastered it, still steaming hot, back on to Jaques' shirt.

'Is that a no?' asked Jaques.

'Our daughter does not answer questions because questions are green and she does not like the colour green,' replied Felicia. 'You know that.'

'I like parks,' said '!'.

'Parks are green,' said Jaques trying to reduce the sneer from his already nasal intonation but not trying very hard.

Felicia walked over to her daughter and sat down beside her.

'!' shifted down the settee, bringing Sir Laurence Olivier, fifty-five tiny bottles of nail polish, five carrier bags full of bows, rags, scraps of material and a pair of red silk ballet pumps which she kept by her side at all times, just in case.

'How did the car get to the park, sweetheart?' asked Felicia.

'!' looked at Sir Laurence Olivier.

'Don't look at me,' thought Sir Laurence Olivier. 'It wasn't my idea, it was hers. It's always her idea. Whoever heard of a dog driving a car?'

'Whoever heard of a dog driving a car?' asked Felicia.

'Exactly,' thought Sir Laurence Olivier.

'Well?' asked Felicia.

'Dog,' said '!'

'Alright, alright, I only did it the once,' thought Sir Laurence Olivier. 'She told me I had to. It would never have entered my mind. Think of the insurance premium, I told her, but she wouldn't listen, "park" she said, "car" she said and before I knew it, I was driving down the A6, listening to *Desert Island Discs* and trying to think of the best way to avoid the lunchtime traffic.'

'So that's settled then, it was the dog. Perhaps we should get him a provisional driving licence?' said Jaques.

'It might be an idea,' thought Sir Laurence Olivier.

'This isn't working,' said Felicia. 'You knew about '!''s issues when you married me. She hasn't changed.'

'No, but you have. Last week you claimed she re-carpeted the spare room,' said Jaques.

'!' looked at Sir Laurence Olivier again who tried not to catch Felicia's eye.

'I know you're her mother but I didn't marry her, I married you.'

Felicia gently reached out to touch her daughter's hand but '!' flinched away. She yearned to be able to hold '!' in her arms, perhaps she could show her daughter what love felt like outside the glass cube '!' had constructed around herself.

'You did marry us, all of us, me, my little girl, my dog. Can't you see how much damage you are doing to her, to all of us?'

'I think you were damaged long before I came along.'

Felicia lifted her hand to stroke her daughter's amber curls but '!' withdrew to the very corner of the settee ensuring that Sir Laurence Olivier was always between her and her mother, between her and the rest of the world. The dog leaned over and licked '!''s face and she played with his ears.

'She lets the dog touch her,' said Felicia, more to herself than to her soon to be ex-partner.

'!' let the dog touch her because she knew that the dog would never hurt her. It was all that she really knew for sure, everything else, her mother, her father, the concept of truth (which was orange), time (which was purple) and love (which was the shape of a dog) were all, would always be, nothing more than an ever-shifting, ever-metamorphosing construct to be worn and put aside but never quite abandoned, like a pair of red silk ballet pumps.

CHAPTER 18

When did the patina of world-weary contempt oxidise onto M's DNA?

If we abseiled down his evolutionary chain would we find a banshee curdling and cursing within his mother's womb?

When he was six, M hid in open sight. He wrote the word 'invisible' across the knuckles of his hands and if he was spoken to he would bring them up to cover his face. It was as if his hands were the curtains to a theatrical performance to which he had never been invited.

In the years before he shot his father almost completely dead, M was a very different entity – insubstantial, opaque. He was cowed because he had no template for self-respect, he was a child who had no access to childhood.

If this was a form of reactive depression (and that was a label that stuck for a while) then it was a manifestation of the world into which he had been unwittingly plunged. It was a world that began and ended each day in turmoil and from which school was a hollow respite. His father surrounded him, screaming down his blood vessels into his brain, swallowing him, consuming him, excreting him.

Can we have empathy for the effigy of the demon if we know that it is fashioned by the cruelty of the stonemason's hands?

*

'What is this evening supposed to be?' asked '!', now an awkward eighteen-year-old girl, with only the most tenuous grasp of reality, who occupied the edge of the high-backed restaurant chair opposite M. M was also eighteen and pretending to be a man but he was convincing no one.

'Because if it is a date of some sort,' she added, 'then you really ought to start speaking.'

'!' surveyed M as if he was an archaeological relic recently unearthed from the sands of the desert. His face was hewn from the finest uncertainty, his eyes were the embers of recently extinguished coals, his mouth was a reminder that better times lay just out of reach. This was a slim M, a lithe M, even muscular in patches, it was an M who offered aggression in the guise of vulnerability.

M fixated upon the blood red cotton tablecloth tracing a solitary vascular thread as it pulsed along its singular course. From time to time he flicked his eyes up at the smile that sat across from him. It reminded him of two stars smashing into each other in the far corner of a distant galaxy. Years later, when love had gone the way of the other dinosaurs, he still felt the same way when she smiled.

They both reached for the single menu that had been abandoned in the centre of the table at the same time and their fingers collided and recoiled.

'Don't touch,' said '!', examining her hand as if she was searching for a bee sting that had just been lodged in it. 'I cannot be touched.'

Given that this was a blind date arranged by their respective consultant psychiatrists, romance was probably unlikely. Survival would have exceeded most expectations. That being said, one would have hoped that 'electively mute' and 'unable to withstand any physical contact whatsoever' might have been mentioned at some point in the matching process.

'Have you ever heard of the child who lived in a bubble?' asked '!'.

M fulminated. All the words had fallen out of his mouth with the sound of the bullet he had fired entering his father's skull. He had searched for them amongst the thoughts which had tumbled out of his father's brain like bloody thorns but they were lost, he assumed, forever.

He shook his head.

'When my mother was born,' '!' explained, 'she was allergic to the world. The Spartans would have had a simple solution, but her parents objected to her being left on a mountainside for the wolves. A scientist in Namibia, Professor Lazarus, had come up with a form of somatic gene therapy which had been successfully used in clinical trials on gazelles and in the absence of any conventional alternative they agreed to let him try it on my mother. A temporary habitat was created – a small bio-globe in her parent's home in the expectation that she wouldn't see out her first year, but she stubbornly refused to die. She kept on growing and growing and they kept adding to the globe until it had taken over their entire home like a giant gerbil run. Everything that went into that globe had to be washed in immuno-therapeutic antigen and this was very expensive and very time-consuming. My grandparents tried to find a way to love my mother but she, quite literally, never touched them. In desperation they went to see Professor Lazarus and he told them what they had known in their hearts on their darkest days; not only was my mother healthier than they were, there was no prospect of her imminent death. Worse still, according to Professor Lazarus, she might never die.

'Eventually, bankrupted and emotionally barren, my grandparents did what any responsible parent of a fifteen-year-old adolescent in a bubble would do – they tied themselves to a grand piano and launched themselves off the top story of the third highest building in Dartford, whilst playing a duet. They took out the bassoon section of the Save the Children marching band. Everyone had an entertaining death that day.

'My mother became something of a minor celebrity and was supported by a combination of charitable donations and media endorsements. At the age of twenty, with nothing on her horizon other than the outlines of boats she could never bring in to focus, my mother wrote off to a sperm bank in Portland, Oregon. She chose a donor from the list, who claimed to have a Postgraduate Masters Degrees in Psychology and Law and in four weeks she had inseminated herself. It was nine months later, on the day I was born, that she discovered that her donor had in fact been the subject of twenty years of psychological study and that the reference to law was as a result of those studies having taken place in a maximum security psychiatric unit in Sing Sing prison.

'I was cut out of my mother like a tumour. She never held me, never kissed me. I was toxic. I wasn't rejected, it was more subtle than that. My mother parented me in the way that she had been parented – with a kind of meticulous distaste. I was fucked up with a degree of creativity rarely seen before by a parent who experienced me as a complicated chattel rather than a child. When the intervention came, when they decided that a child who had gnawed through her own knuckles to the bone might be in need of a little time out from her mother, all that was left of me was a knotted ball of wool that could never be unravelled. Add to that the traits I have inherited from a father who was imprisoned at the age of sixteen for murdering five semi-professional ballroom dancers whilst wearing the recently emptied skull of a wildebeest and you have the perfect dinner date.'

M had begun to perspire. There was an unfamiliar movement within his chest cavity, he thought he was going to be sick, but what came out of his mouth was the end of a sentence he had started to speak eight years earlier.

'Stop,' he rasped and slumped back into his chair exhausted.

'!' stopped.

'Have you ever seen the way a cat tortures a small bird?' asked M. 'Never letting it get far away, desperately gentle, programmed to preserve life in order to destroy it. That was my father. Each day his criticism would kill us a little more, tiny loving wounds delivered by a man with endless ammunition. We were all damaged in different ways but it was intangible. Teachers, therapists, counsellors couldn't get to the bottom of it; they couldn't see that all myself and my siblings were, all we are, are tiny birds, waiting for the certainty of the final deadly blow.'

He was waiting for '!' to leave and inside she certainly wanted to, but this was the '!' who would one day become M's wife before the unbearable knowledge that she was a mermaid weighed down upon her until she could barely move.

'!' reached out a hand and placed it close to M's on the table.

'Do you think you could kiss me without touching?' she asked.

M had never kissed anyone before but was sure that touching was the point of the exercise. And yet, he thought, and yet, perhaps this would be better.

'I could try,' he said.

CHAPTER 19

Residing in us all is the stubborn spark of perfection. It may be incongruous to the geography of our DNA, but it is this and this alone which fills our lungs with breath each day.

*

As he lay in bed each morning, Dorsal Grellman would study the tattered photograph taken through the window of the small local pub his parents once frequented. It was an image of a world from the time before their relationship ruptured, causing them to haemorrhage their son. He would linger, transfixed by the image of his mother and father fussing over his infant self. He wanted to be part of that beloved triumvirate, to understand how this nascent Dorsal had felt, to know he belonged, was entangled. He had been too young to learn the vocabulary of love and now he was illiterate. 'Reach out', he implored this static two dimensional Dorsal and then, beset by the malady of betrayal, he would put away the photograph until the next day. It was his only deviation from the path of violence and it was a ritual performed for fear that his last connection with the past might shatter and with it the last vestige of his humanity.

Abandonment had left him conflicted – it was this photograph that reminded him about the infinite capacity of parents to make their children suffer and stoked the malodorous flames of his antipathy for them.

*

'He's done it again, head teacher,' said Mrs Phibes, the woman cursed with bestowing art upon the heathen of Camden, the most northerly outpost of what had once been the Holy Roman Empire, whose ruthless, all conquering, despotic mantle had now been bestowed upon the Inner London Education Authority.

Caldwell Bynes, who retained the helm of The D'Oily Cart Academy for boys despite remaining resolutely anti-child and anti-education, regarded the telephone as if it were contaminated with leprosy. He was a man who experienced hatred in the same way that others felt hunger. He had, for a while, worn surgical gloves to shield him from human contact, having once been so appalled by a parent whose hands had consumed his own like a ravenous alligator that he had vomited on them. When the cloying feel of the latex began to disgust him he resolved to become a recluse, meeting other members of his species for the sole purpose of administering punishment and disseminating wretchedness. In this, he had achieved Olympian proficiency.

'What have you done with it, Mrs Phibes?'

'I've put it out with the rubbish just as you told me to do with the others, head teacher.'

Bynes looked at his hands – an archaeological spider's web of furrows and ridges had begun to radiate up his arms like the traces of a physiological radar signal. This was evidence of ageing at its most villainous, pickpocketing the years and leaving him bereft of time.

'And the boy knows nothing, Mrs Phibes?'

'I have told him that his paintings are an abomination, head teacher, just as you instructed me, and yet…'

Defiance? Bynes ran the Academy with a Stalinist ethos. There was no room for dissidents or exile; they were already in Siberia. Teachers were members of his secret police force, Stasi officers who were expected to inform on each other and submit to his absolute authority or pay the ultimate price. It was roughly in line with National Schooling Guidelines, with a few tweaks.

'Are you questioning me, Mrs Phibes?' His words twisted back and forth in the icy gale they had manifested.

'No, head teacher,' replied Mrs Phibes, clearly shaken by the suggestion.

'Because if this is a challenge to my authority…you will recall what happened to Mr Herald. I doubt that the stains will ever come out of the walls of the geography lecture theatre.'

'It's just that he is such an exceptional young artist, what a shame to…'

'He is an enforcer, a hired gun, a hoodlum, a goon and under no circumstances whatsoever is he permitted to be talented in anything other than administering indiscriminate malfeasance at my bidding and whim. If he does it again, burn it in the classroom in his face and send him to me. I will deal with him.'

Colin Collins, professor emeritus of the Ruskin School of Drawing and Fine Art, University of Oxford, had found a hairstyle which suited him, by chance, at 6.45pm on the 18th March 1976 and had never been able to recapture it. His head, at best, sported what appeared to be the ruins of a Mayan temple constructed out of Asian palm civet faeces. At worst, it was as though two crows had waged a battle to the death and their remains had been covered in bitumen and ignited.

Dressed in a full-length green velveteen cape and leatherette codpiece, Colin Collins was very much a man of his time and that time was the late sixteenth century.

Finding himself, if not in the arse end of London, then certainly in its nether regions, Collins covered his nose alternately with a lace kerchief and a posy of roses. Positing that the stench might overpower him, he gripped a vial of smelling salts as he entered the tawdry precincts of what was officially the school with the worst overall academic record in Southern England – The D'Oily Cart Academy. (The school with the second worst academic record had recently been burnt down by its own headmaster but whilst only the smouldering ruins remained, it still scored a higher satisfaction rating amongst children and parents than 'The Cart'.)

Acting on a tip-off from an anonymous source, Collins made his way to the giant metal bins at the rear of the science building where he found, underneath a steaming pile of duck beaks and what appeared to be a human hand, a battered artist's portfolio. He undid the gnarled ribbon with trembling fingers. He imagined how Howard Carter might have felt as he entered the tomb of Tutankhamen and, brushing away the last remnants of duck, he opened the portfolio.

The paintings dazzled him like a ray of sunlight slicing its way through the musty inner sanctum of a church crypt. Redolent of a young Caravaggio, this was a master's hand. He searched for a signature or a date, how could the work of a genius have been consigned to this ignominy. He turned over the first painting for a clue and found a rectangular sticker. The manuscript inscription read, 'Your work is far too pretentious – you were asked to depict "what you did on holiday" and according to the title of this painting, "The Slaughter of the Three Wise Men by the Beast During a Visit to a Cocktail Bar in Margate", this would appear to be a matter for Special Branch, the Vatican and the Licensing department of Thanet District Council. "F" fail – Bynes C, Head Teacher.'

There were similar stickers on the other works. A spectacular oil painting titled 'The Beheading of Anne Boleyn by a Traffic Warden Just Outside the Newly Refurbished Offices of Newport Pagnell Rural District Council' bore all the hallmarks of Velasquez. The sticker on its reverse read, 'This would have been a flagrant breach of the secretary of states guidelines for the conduct of parking attendants and traffic related operatives – section 6.13.4 – unprovoked acts of violence perpetrated against members or putative members of the House of Tudor. "F" fail – Bynes C, Head Teacher.'

There had been no greater crime against the international art and cultural community since *The Hymnes of Astraea* had a disappointing first publication in 1599 or Van Morrison was removed from the Rock and Roll Hall of Fame and Colin Collins would have no truck with it. He would track down this Bynes C, expose him as the charlatan and mountebank he clearly was and discover the identity of this artistic prodigy whose talents had been so outlandishly suppressed. He departed the bin store with a lavish swish of his cape. He liked a good swish.

*

'There is someone to see you, headmaster,' growled Mrs Bennett, Bynes' redoubtable PA, through the mouthpiece of her semi-functional telephone, her voice almost lost amidst a minefield of static. 'He appears to have been waiting since the early part of the sixteenth century.'

Collins swept into Bynes' office, slammed the portfolio down on his palatial desk and stood with one foot on the visitor's chair, his hands on his hips and his codpiece thrust forwards for maximum dramatic effect.

'And?' asked Bynes quizzically.

'Are you the ignoramus who has decried this pre-eminent work so scandalously?' asked Collins with Shakespearean aplomb.

'Go fuck yourself,' said Bynes.

'I am Colin Collins, professor emeritus of the Ruskin School of Drawing and Fine Art, University of Oxford – I sponsored Hockney in his first exhibition in the United Kingdom, I am a pre-eminent expert in the work of Millais and was a confidant of Warhol, I have been the senior judge for the Royal Academy summer exhibition for the last twenty-five years. How dare you speak to me in that way, you shrivelled, pasty-faced, weasel of a man?'

'I am so sorry,' said Bynes, 'there appears to have been a terrible misunderstanding.'

'I am glad to hear it,' replied Collins, brushing imaginary stagecoach dust from his knee.

'Go fuck yourself Professor Collins, you unutterably emeritus shite hazard,' said Bynes. 'Is that a bit better?'

'Your puerile abuse is of no consequence to me. I want to know what qualifies you to judge this man's work?' bristled Collins, brandishing his lace kerchief at Bynes as aggressively as one can brandish a lace kerchief.

'Dorsal Grellman to the head teacher's office right away,' Bynes demanded, through the prehistoric school-wide intercom.

Bynes and Collins sat in silence for a moment before thunderous foot-falls approached along the western corridor, shaking the variety of totemic ephemera that littered Bynes' desk from their dusty resting places. Collins was in fear that a large predatory animal had muscled out of its zoo cage and was set to devour them and he was not dissuaded from this when Dorsal burst into the study with Ferris still under his arm in a headlock. Collins raised his hands instinctively to his face to prevent scarring. It was the standard knee-jerk reaction experienced by anyone meeting Dorsal for the first time.

'This is your young auteur, Professor Collins, is he what you antici-pated?'

'His appearance is immaterial,' replied Collins unconvincingly, 'genius is blind. He will bring the world of art to its knees, he will be the figurehead of a new Renaissance.'

Bynes sat back in his chair with a comfortable squeak and interlaced his fingers.

'That's not what he's for, Professor Collins.'

'For...' replied Collins.

'When I bought him from his parents it was not for his artistic potential,' said Bynes. 'He is, will always be, a thug, my thug. This artistic streak needs to be stamped out, not encouraged by some ageing sycophantic relic from the court of Henry the Eighth. He will not be permitted to paint anything again, his art teacher will see to that. Now if it's no inconve-nience I would like him to beat the living shite out of you and then burn his artwork so that this never happens again. Dorsal, if you wouldn't mind.'

But Dorsal did mind. He was not aware that his parents had profited from his enslavement to Bynes, that they had travelled so very far from love. This man thought his art was good, great, that he had value, purpose, that he was more than the dust that Bynes ground his face into.

'Thinking about leaving me, Dorsal – where are you going to go? Professor Collins, can Dorsal come and live with you in Never-Never Land, he's almost house trained now?'

'Well, I, it's, I don't have…' flustered Collins.

'No, no one has the space for a child who smells like a bison on heat, requires a nine foot-long bed and is liable to decapitate you if you don't get his eggy soldiers right in the morning. Funny that. You hear that Grellman, no one will have you, you are lucky that I put up with you and your ugly ways but you fulfil a function and whilst you continue to do so you will have a place here.'

'He is not an animal and you should not speak to him as if he is, he is a child,' said Collins.

'He is neither,' replied Bynes, 'he is a symptom of a disease for which there has never been a name. He will never inherit the earth, he will never raise the eagle standard above his head in triumph, he is the machinery of vengeance and he is mine. Now deal with Professor Collins and return to what you were made for. There is no room for aspiration in this world, only duty, everything else is artifice.'

Dorsal turned from Bynes and shook with a pain that knew no remorse. As he dealt with Colin Collins, his eyes ragged with tears, he knew that he was the night.

CHAPTER 20

Monday morning and still not murdered, Daniel entered the school playground to find a line of twenty or more children of various ages snaking
across his path. Some weeks before, Dorsal Grellman had informed the
head teacher that he was finding his job both time-consuming and unre-
warding. It seemed that not only were many of the recipients of his peculiar
brand of violence ungrateful but also, in some cases, surprisingly evasive.

By initiating a queuing system the head teacher believed that bullying
could be conducted in an orderly manner each morning, giving Dorsal the
opportunity to pursue his hobby of torturing members of the teaching staff,
at his leisure, throughout the rest of the day.

A ginger-haired child whose features were covered by a dense thicket
of freckles stepped forwards impassively, handed Dorsal the contents of
his pockets and was punched in the head, knocking him off his feet into a
puddle. He stood up, brushed himself down and walked into school snivel-
ling.

A hushed silence fell when the next child stepped forwards. He was
wearing two pairs of glasses and appeared from almost every angle to be
perfectly rectangular. He handed Dorsal a tattered 'Dungeons and Dragons'
playing card and tried to initiate a polite conversation.

'This is an ancient wizarding token which gives you the right to enter the
Kingdom of Kalamar. There you will find your elf guide who will take you
to the Inn of the Screaming Elms where you must ask for Gwendrach the
Goblin King – it is he and only he who can...'

It was difficult for Ferris to continue speaking because by this point he
was lying in a puddle with Dorsal's shoe in his mouth. Dorsal used his
fingertips to reach down into Ferris' jacket pocket and remove a packet of
chocolate buttons which he poured into his palm and swallowed all at once.

Dorsal stood on Ferris' head and grabbed the little girl who was next in the queue by the pony tails when it occurred to him that breathing, which he had excelled at up to that point in time, was no longer as straightforward as it had once seemed. It had in fact become completely impossible. The chocolate buttons had formed a cork which had lodged in his trachea and he was about to suffer an ironic death.

Dorsal fell to his knees in the puddle clutching his throat. Unfortunately for Ferris, the current incumbent of the puddle, this meant that Dorsal's full weight was now on his perfectly rectangular buttocks and head leaving him with no option other than to drown. Daniel, who had been following these events from a safe distance, mustered his tiny legs into a sprint and with the assistance of the little girl with pony tails and nine other children, he was able to shift Dorsal (whose face had assumed a hue of fire engine red which is particularly popular with interior decorators) and pull Ferris free. Ferris leapt to his feet, retrieved both pairs of muddied spectacles and grabbing Dorsal by the waist he delivered five perfect upward thrusts into his abdomen, dislodging the chocolate and allowing Dorsal to breathe again.

It did not surprise Daniel that Ferris, an eight-year-old child, knew how to perform the Heimlich manoeuvre – he also knew how to defuse a thermo nuclear warhead and how to take off his pants without removing his trousers. What surprised him was that Ferris had chosen to save the life of Dorsal Grellman.

*

There are four hundred and ninety-three different Pokémon figurines and Ferris had every single one, in its original box. Each one was pristine, never played with and in that way, never understood. This was not a collection; it was something far, far worse. Daniel had never seen anything like Ferris' bedroom but he had never seen anything like Ferris before so the bedroom was no real surprise.

The removal of the father section from the structure once described as Ferris' parents had left the remaining mother section cruelly exposed to the elements. Love, demonstrative affection, empathy, had all been his father's department. His mother had supplied business integrity and financial acumen – not exactly essential parental attributes – and when his father died even these deserted her. She gave and she gave and yet Ferris received nothing and needed everything. She had become his almost-mother and the love she had once felt for her son had taken a one-way caravan holiday to Newquay.

The sense of gratitude that she had felt towards Daniel – at last a child who would befriend the un-befriendable Ferris – was unbounded. Daniel was the torch-bearer in a home that had lost all sense of light, he was the four hundred and ninety-fourth Pokémon and she didn't plan to let him leave anytime soon. If Daniel found the look of unabashed murderous hatred he saw every day in the eyes of his father, of his headmaster, of pretty much everyone he met, disconcerting, it was at least something he understood. The look of unfettered propriety in Ferris' mother's eyes was far more frightening.

Daniel sat in the chair which Ferris and his mother had decorated for his first after-school visit. The legs and arms had been wrapped in silver foil and a red velvet curtain had been taken down from their lounge window and laid across the seat and chair back. To many it might have appeared to be a throne.

Ferris was experiencing a level of karmic fulfilment hitherto attained only by Dalai Lamas. He had a friend in his bedroom perhaps not playing with, but certainly experiencing his toys and it had not, as yet, been neces-sary to physically restrain him in order to prevent him from leaving. He stared out of the window, his street had been daubed in vivid colours he had never witnessed before – the front door of the house opposite his, the white cat which lay sleeping on the car in his neighbour's drive, the poplar tree, Dorsal Grellman, the daffodils growing in the window box of the…

It occurred to Ferris that the view from his window now contained one Dorsal Grellman more than it had done hitherto and it was walking towards his front door.

A few moments later, Ferris' mother entered his bedroom ululating with emotion. Dorsal stood directly behind her. Daniel could not immediately see a weapon but that did not mean that there wasn't one.

'This is Dorsal,' she rasped, 'he says he's your…'

'Friend,' said Dorsal, throwing her against the wall affectionately and entering the bedroom.

'I'm their friend.'

CHAPTER 21

Ferris' mother passed Daniel a plate piled high with giant home-made fairy cakes that had been dipped in hundreds and thousands. Daniel regarded them with abject horror before shaking his head. They were not intended to be inedible but since no one had ever eaten one, it was the same thing. It was Sunday teatime and Daniel had become a fixture in Ferris' home. Provided he ate nothing, Daniel had found a place that was safe.

'What was my father like?' asked Ferris.

Ferris' mother regarded her son as if he was an alien who had spoken to her for the first time, in a language she had no hope of ever comprehending.

'Your father was everything to you, he cooked every meal you ate, taught you to read and write, how to ride a bicycle, how to fly a kite. When you were ill, he was first with a diagnosis or solution, he tucked you into bed at night and took you to school in the morning. He was present during every one of your key developmental milestones, he held you when you cried, bathed you, dried you and taught you what he perceived to be the difference between wrong and not quite so wrong.'

'And all of that was a good thing?' asked Ferris.

His mother picked up a fairy cake, it was the size of her fist. She raised her hand and dropped it onto the dining room table where it landed with a corpse-like thud. 'Once you were born you became his alpha and his omega. He gave up his scientific research, he gave up his friends, he ceased to be a husband or a man, he was defined solely by paternity. Your father left no space for anyone else in his relationship with you and so when he decided to die four years ago, we were cut adrift. I supported you both and yet, because of him, I was no more relevant to you than the postman.'

'You allowed him to do this,' said Ferris, 'you allowed yourself to become a margin – a footnote.'

'It is never as simple as that, Ferris. You do not always know you have been defeated at the time that it happens. It's often only in retrospect that you realise that you have been in a battle with winners and losers – that you have, somehow, been defeated.'

'So how is it I have only a handful of memories of him, all of them negative?' asked Ferris. 'I need more, I have a right to have more.'

'These are the vagaries of the wiring of the human brain, Ferris. We have no choice in what is indelible and what is erased. Even when we win the race it may only be the cold black metal of the starter's pistol that we recall. Your father left us, he is still leaving us every day. He casts a shadow on our home that all the light in the world cannot illuminate. So you want to know what your father was like. He was a loving, caring, devoted and generous parent but more than that, more than anything and in perpetuity, he was an infamously pathetic shite-magnet.'

Neither boy was fazed by this, they had heard worse, experienced worse on a daily basis.

'My father hates me, he has been present at every important moment in my life to ensure that no one made it any more enjoyable than it needed to be,' said Daniel.

'I have spoken with your father,' replied Ferris' mother calmly, 'he doesn't hate you, he wants you dead, it's not the same thing at all.'

'How, how could you…' said Daniel.

'It was at one of Mr Bynes' open evenings for parents who have a somewhat problematic, err, relationship with their…'

'It's for parents who want to kill their children,' said Ferris.

It was his mother's turn to be shocked.

'Don't worry, I know it isn't personal,' said Ferris. 'You have no idea what to do with me and you have been looking at your options.'

'I have never actually contemplated, wouldn't really have…' struggled his mother.

'Can I show you something?' asked Ferris. 'It might not make you proud exactly but it may suggest to you a number of ways in which I could be commercially exploited.'

At last his mother smiled at him. He was playing her song.

CHAPTER 22

The attic room in Ferris' home – what had been his father's laboratory – was a maelstrom of rubber pipes, bunsen burners, petri dishes, centrifuges and cages containing assorted rodents. All of the interconnected tubing led to a single small glass tank in the centre of the room, which was sitting on heated pads.

'Haven't you wondered what I have been up to all these months in dad's old laboratory and what I was doing with the animals you supplied me with?' asked Ferris.

'I hoped you were torturing them, I am sure they deserved it,' replied Ferris' mother.

Ferris flicked on a central switch and the ceiling lights in the room pulsed. He walked over to the glass tank, disconnected it and handed it to his mother.

'I have been working on this project for the last two years. There were a few scientific and moral hurdles to overcome but last week this happened,' said Ferris.

His mother held the tank up to her eyes.

'A goldfish happened?' she asked.

'Take a closer look,' said Ferris.

She looked into the tank again. There was a small amphibian creature swimming around it in cloudy water. It was not a creature she was familiar with.

She looked up at Ferris and back to the creature. 'You ought to change this water, it's a bit cloudy.'

'It's amniotic fluid,' explained Ferris. 'Oppenheimer speculated that man was his own creator, that there was an incestuous synchronicity in evolution. The key to life itself has remained elusive, its pursuit anachronistic, some might say, perverse. But examining my father's research into exogenesis it occurred to me that a common origin of everything, from blades of grass to imploding dwarf stars might dwell inside us all. I took some of the raw cellular material from the reproductive organs of rats, mice, birds and fish and compared it on a sub-molecular level with the stamen of flowers. I exposed them to extremes of temperature, to vacuums and controlled micro nuclear explosions and whilst I found some community in the structural displacement of the DNA there was nothing that resembled a baseline, particularly when compared with what we know about the formation of stars.

'I was searching for Pandora's box in a submicroscopic valley of the kings but the truth wasn't hidden within the lungs of a Sphinx but inside a grain of sand. What lies within the phial that will unlock both a gas giant and a razorback clam? I challenged myself to find the least likely solution and by the purest chance, three months ago, it found me. There is a jewel chiselled from a single shard of antimatter. A piece of that jewel lies within everything. It was inside the car park that Daniel's father made him descend, it is inside the lions that swim within your veins and it was inside this creature in this bowl when I made it.'

Ferris' mother replaced the tank carefully, put her arm around her son and squeezed him to her.

'So, what you are trying to tell me, is that, at the age of eight, you have created life in our attic,' she said, 'and this is it?'

She smiled broadly and kissed the moss patch of brown hair on top of his head. 'No one is going to believe you.'

'My father was a nuclear physicist, my mother is a research biochemist, it's not beyond the realms of possibility that...'

'Oh, I think it is sunshine, there's no fucking way that anyone is going to accept that you came up with the most important discovery in the history of the human race. You, a snot infested Star Wars-obsessed child who can barely reach the toilet flush.'

Ferris was beginning to shake, tears were lipping over the floodgates of his eyes. 'But Daniel knows – he knows...'

'Daniel, is that it? It's hardly corroboration by the International Military Tribunal at Nuremberg is it? I think the massed ranks of the world's press and the Nobel Prize panel are going to need something a bit more substantial than the word of your rather pathetic friend here, as grateful as I am to him. No, I think it is fair to say that mummy is very clever and you are a very proud little man. Now sod off to your bedroom,' she ushered Daniel and Ferris from the laboratory, 'go play with Luke Skywalker and Hans Solo while I work out what to wear for my interview with the *International Herald Tribune*.'

*

An hour later, when the tears had finally subsided, Daniel sidled up to Ferris on his bed and offered him half of a Kit Kat.

'We need to leave, you and I, leave here,' said Ferris 'we need to find somewhere that is ours. We aren't needed here and we aren't safe.'

'I always thought you enjoyed adversity,' said Daniel.

'I enjoy attention,' said Ferris 'it's just that it's always associated with pain and disassociated with love.'

'We can't leave,' said Daniel 'not until this is over. If I am to become my parents as they became my grandparents, then I need to understand why.'

CHAPTER 23

The incident that led to M's less than symbiotic relationship with food occurred on the day of his wedding to the woman who was to become Daniel's mother.

The logistics of arranging for the transportation of M's mother-in-law in her bubble were complex enough, but the security required for his psychotically deviant American sperm donor father-in-law did rob the occasion of some of its romantic sparkle. Then there was the issue of Bernice, M's mother. M was certain that the lack of any guests who were major characters from the world of science fiction would ensure that she did not feel compelled to off anyone before the best man's speech, but she was still about as safe around the general public as a hand grenade without its pin.

M had few other relatives to invite – there were of course apologies for the absence of his father – not surprising given that M believed he had executed him, Mafia-style, on the day of his twelfth birthday. M's brother Clive and sister Bathsheba – or 'uncle drunk' and 'auntie mad' as they came to be known – were more than enough family for anyone.

Since M and his fiancée had no room for friends or social graces within the imploding dwarf stars which masqueraded as their lives, it fell to Clive and Bathsheba to organise the wedding. They embarked on the project with great vigour, never previously having been entrusted with anything more demanding than wiping their own arses and within a week they had identified a venue.

'It looks like the South Mimms service station at the intersection of the M25 and the M1 just north of Watford,' said M, nervously thumbing through the photographs he had been supplied with.

'It isn't,' replied Clive.

'That's good,' replied M.

'It's the triangle of wasteland formed by the intersection of the two motorways, across the hard shoulder and crash barrier behind the service station,' Clive explained.

'I see,' said M. He was shaking in the way that lions do before a kill – that ecstatic inner waltz in anticipation of an act of violence that is so pure, it is almost exotic. He knew that allowing his brother and sister (people he often hurt but would never harm) to assume the pivotal role in what would be an event of unparalleled importance in his life was essential if he was to avoid an overly punitive response to disappointment. M was like a blind man, but it was empathy rather than vision which he lacked. His brain had compensated for this deficit by developing an indiscriminate loathing for all of the human race

'Why? asked M, his hands opening and closing as if he were a marionette in a livid puppet show.

'I love cars,' replied Bathsheba, earnestly. 'Have you ever really looked at a spinning car tyre – they all resonate at different speeds, sending sparks into the air that are the colour of passion and treachery. They will lead a rainbow of sprites on a path over your heads as you give your vows and they will tie a web of golden jeopardy around your wrists which cannot be broken by the harlots of time.'

'Although parking might be a bit of a problem,' added Clive.

M breathed through his nose. He wondered if his brother and sister's heads would fit inside a vacuum cleaner.

'As wonderful as this sounds,' said M, 'I was looking for something a little more…conventional.'

'What if we chose a different stretch of motorway?' asked Bathsheba, crestfallen.

'No motorways, no cars, I want an ordinary building accessible by road with a nice garden, a decent bar and toilet facilities,' said M.

'Does such a place even exist?' whispered Bathsheba as Clive led her away by her bejewelled arm. 'I suppose it must,' replied Clive in disbelief.

*

M's bride to be sat on her bed, staring at her reflection in a mirror that had witnessed her face grow from tortured youth to bereft adulthood. It was her face that offered the context for change – the mirror remained the same – grey, opaque, kissed by the light from the window that was always just out of frame – as did her expression – loss, lost.

She ran her fingers along the spine of her journal, hard, green, replete with years of awkward ruminations. She opened it at the latest entry, titled *The 10 things I hate most about M.*

1. I believe he is planning to kill the President of the United States of America with an axe – a sharpened golf club would also do the job. This would have to be at close range. I have no evidence to corroborate this but he looks like the type who might.

2. I have woken late at night to find him standing by the window in the nude. He has a diagonal scar from one side of his chest to the other – he runs his finger along its length as if it is a musical instrument. He will not tell me how it happened, only that the person who did it is dead and he killed him.

3. I love him.

4. He took me to Raynham Hall for my twenty-second birthday and he watched the staircase intently for nine hours in case we saw 'a misty form.' He did not go to the toilet. He did not buy a sandwich despite being offered one on three occasions by the woman from the British Legion. When he was asked to leave he demanded his money back and when the guide refused, M dragged him into the toilet and stuck his head down it until the man apologised for not providing a ghostly apparition. He did not wish me happy birthday. There was no cake. There were no balloons.

5. Everything must be in fives. Five is very important to me. It is the number that stops the shouting when it is at its worst. M deliberately sorted everything in our bathroom into groups of four. In response to this I smashed him in the face repeatedly with a flowering cactus (*Cumulopuntia Boliviana*). This was not good for the cactus.

6. He has told me that I am more of a prisoner than my mother who lives in a bubble. This is true but he has the key to my cell and he will never let me out.

7. His favourite film is *It's a Wonderful Life*. He has watched this film over 3000 times and he has made me watch it over 100 times. Each time he watches it he cries continuously and does not stop crying until he falls asleep snoring. He will not tell me why this is. Last night, we watched *It's a Wonderful Life* twice and during the second viewing I recited the entire script along with the characters, assuming their voices. My Donna Reed and my Lionel Barrymore could do with some work, but I believe my impersonation of James Stewart is uncanny. M told me to stop and when I refused, he waited until the

end of the film, kicked in the television and was sick down himself before falling asleep on the sofa. This is not the way I envisaged I would be spending the night before my wedding although it was fairly close to it.

8. We are getting married on the main concourse of Cliftonville Railway station. M explained that this was (a) because his sister liked trains (b) that this was as good as it was going to get and he had rejected his brother and sister's other ideas which included runway number 3 at Stansted Airport, the landing site of Apollo 11 in the Sea of Tranquility on the Moon, the Bridge on the River Kwai and Hull (c) there are excellent toilet and catering facilities and (d) according to his sister Bathsheba, trains sing to you at night with the voices of the children who live in the waves.

9. I think that his father broke him in a way that can never be fixed. You could reassemble M but there would always be three pieces left on the side which you could find no use for; these would be his conscience, his sense of morality and his ability to experience happiness.

10. I fear for us if we were to have a child but most of all, I fear for the child.

She stood, put her journal away in a drawer she would never open again, straightened her wedding dress and made her way towards the rest of her life. There was a single word written on the journal, it was 'romance.'

CHAPTER 24

'I have a very special wedding present for you,' said Bernice, M's mother. 'You won't like it.'

They were standing in the waiting room on Platform 3 of Cliftonville Railway Station. Clive and Bathsheba had insisted that the guests should not observe what they had described as 'Shangri-La meets the 1435mm standard gauge railway system' until the finishing touches were complete. The station manager had become so distressed when shown the advance sketches of Clive and Bathsheba's 'graphic vision' for the main concourse that he had become doubly incontinent. It had been necessary for M to pop him down to the local A & E to select a 'pick and mix' of disabling injuries should he remain demur, before the function was given the green light.

Adjusting M's cravat in a proprietorial manner, Bernice sighed. This rudderless craft, careening blindly down life's waterways, leaving one fatal collision after another in its wake, was all her own work. She had borne him for nine long months, shat him out and watched him melt under the wicked gaze of his father, without lifting a finger to stop the party. What more could you ask of a parent?

Bernice was wearing a full length amber velour evening dress and walked with the swagger of a victorious barbarian raider. She removed a small square present wrapped in hessian, bound in a silk bow entwined with razor wire from her handbag and handed it, carefully, to M. It was a golden framed photograph of a man who could bleed you dry without opening his mouth.

'You remember your father, I hope?' enquired Bernice.

'When I was five he tried to cook my brother and I on a barbecue. I went through ten years of intensive weekly psychotherapy after blowing a hole in his head with the gun he gave me as a birthday present, a gun that you let him give me. I still have waking and sleeping nightmares about him – last night I dreamt that the hole in his demolished head sprouted teeth and tried to eat me, so yes, I do remember my fucking father,' replied M.

'Yes, yes,' said Bernice, 'whatever, anyway, this is my present to you.'

'A picture of my dead father.'

'Well, this is a picture of him not being quite so dead,' replied Bernice. 'It was taken last week.'

M looked at the photograph again.

'Am I pissing on your parade?' asked Bernice.

M could not breathe. He sat down heavily onto the floor in the corner of the waiting room amidst the souls of a million dust bunnies.

'The wall was covered with globules of his brain, a shard of his skull lodged in Bathsheba's hip and had to be dug out,' said M, 'how can he be...'

'You were catatonic, you were always such a lightweight, you don't know what you saw. I scooped up all the bits of head gunk that looked important into a lunchbox with a bit of ice – I always knew that the Girl Guide training would come in handy – grappled him into the boot of the car and we all went on a nice trip to see Dr Mark-with-a-CK. If you are going to make an opium addled, cross-dressing, struck-off brain surgeon the godparent of your children you might as well get the best possible use out of him, I always think.

'While the three of you were screaming sweet nothings in the car, Dr Mark-with-a-CK was proving that you can put Humpty Dumpty together again, although possibly not in the right order. I told you all that daddy had gone to Hades but he was in Hackney, running a cafe all this time. He was a cunt with half a brain and three children before you shot him and he was a cunt with half a brain and a cafe in Hackney after you shot him. If anything, you did him a favour.'

'This is...' M did not know what it was, it felt like his hands were stopping his head from falling off.

'Evil,' replied Bernice. 'Well here's a newsflash, old sport, I'm not very nice, it's our collective DNA, it's like a family tradition. We should have written it on the little tag that was sewn into the back of your school jumper instead of your name. You can run away from it as fast as your little legs will carry you but you will still keep arriving back at the same place – Bastard on Thames.'

Bernice crouched down so that her face was inches away from M's.

'You are so much like your father,' she whispered, 'you have his sensibility and his insatiably cruel hands. Oh and just before I go, because I'm not hanging around to see the Mardi Gras of shite your brother and sister have conjured up for your wedding day, I have a little prediction. One day when you have a child, M, a child who is not loved despite your indefatigable capacity to love, a child like you, your father, Jonah, will come to your door and you will open it and let him in. He will want to speak to your child and you will let him. Until then, don't get too preoccupied by this happiness thing – it won't last.'

With this, Bernice swept off into the embrace of her very own perfidious Albion, never to enter into M's orbit again.

*

The bride threaded her arm through Clive's at the double doors leading to the station concourse. Her prospective brother-in-law was dressed in what could best be described as 'period noir'.

'Is that human blood?' asked the bride, pointing an expensively manicured cuticle at Clive's crimson spattered dress shirt. 'No, no, no,' giggled Clive, 'human blood, no, of course not.' He opened the doors allowing her to greet the audacious horror he had knitted from strands of reality. 'It's pig's blood,' he said, leading her down the 'aisle' towards her gaping guests.

*

'It's an abattoir,' hissed M as he and his sister entered the thronged, white silken pavilion which his siblings had erected on the concourse. His guests sat on either side of the interior, flanked by tall poles, and at the far end was the altar, which had been constructed out of small cages. Atop each of the poles was a dripping pig's head.

'It's not an abattoir, it's a charnel house,' sighed Bathsheba proudly.

When the bride arrived at the entrance to the pavilion on Clive's arm, Bathsheba raised her hand and each of the pig's heads burst into flames. Fat perspired down the poles onto the ground in pools.

M's siblings had dispensed with traditional music to accompany the bride. As she advanced, the mice in the cages which made up the altar, all of whom had been mic'ed up to speakers, began twilling and chirruping in unison as an undulating electrical charge pulsed through them. The noise was a stomach-churning cacophony.

When the bride reached M's side, Clive released a brace of white doves to whose feet the wedding rings had been tied. They fluttered above the heads of the guests until Bathsheba released the hawk. In seconds the rings had fallen to the ground at the bride's slippered feet amongst still trembling dove miscellany.

A number of guests screamed but it was difficult to be certain exactly how many because most of them were already crying.

The registrar had observed these events unfold before her eyes distractedly. This was partially because she had been marrying people for over forty years and was not easily surprised but mainly because her leg had been chained to a tiger. The tiger had been heavily dosed with cannabis but it had begun to lick the registrar's foot in a way that might have been either loving or tasting, it was difficult to say which.

'Dearly-beloved-we-are-gathered-here-today-for-the-marriage-of-these-two-people,' said the registrar with tiger-related rapidity. 'Any objections? No, rings on fingers, good, do-you-take-him, yep, you-her-right – I hereby-declare…'

'Stop,' shouted the bride. 'This is my fucking wedding day. Mine. Never mind the burning pig's heads and the tiger and the amplified mouse singing and the dove slaughter. Never mind the commuters gawping and the guests throwing up on themselves and my imaginary mother in the bubble and my killer sperm donor father. This is the day that I marry the man that I love, the beautiful man that I love.' She took M's hand. 'And none of this bullshit is going to get in the way of that.'

'Are those your vows, because if they are if we can just wrap this up, I need to…' said the Registrar who had sensed, more than heard, a low menacing growl emanating from the floor near to her feet.

'No they aren't my fucking vows,' screamed the bride.

'M, you have been a terrible boyfriend. You are ill mannered to the point of obsession, a poor conversationalist, a clumsy, perfunctory lover and possibly the most impatient living thing since life first scrambled out of the primordial soup. But when I look into your eyes, when I really look, I know that you are the place I need to be.'

M lifted his bride's veil and for a moment, sobs clotted his throat.

'When I'm with you,' said M, 'the screaming in my heart stops. I can find a path through the savagery that claims me and seek sanctuary. I love you for what you have shown me I could be and whatever happens to stain that love as the hours turn to tears, it will always, in some form, endure.'

The bride looked at the ring that M had placed on her finger. Encrusted into the top in diamonds was a number 5.

'Fives are really important,' said M's wife, a single tear working its way timidly out of the corner of her eye.

'I know they are,' replied M, smiling with all the strength that he possessed.

'You-are-now-declared-husband-and-wife-you-may-kiss-the-bride, now get this tiger off my fucking ankle,' said the Registrar.

The kiss was a moment of true honesty for M and his wife, which was only replicated when they stood together in silence as M held their dead son Saul in his arms.

'I'm suddenly ravenous,' said M. 'I feel as if I haven't eaten anything my whole life and I need to start right now and never stop.'

And he never did.

CHAPTER 25

The 'gut-buster breakfast' at the Belvedere Cafe in Fetter Lane consisted of fifteen eggs, twelve sausages, ten rashers of bacon, twenty-two slices of fried toast, five black pudding slices, a catering-sized tin of baked beans and a tomato. op had chosen the slimline option which omitted the tomato and was in the process of licking his empty plate clean. He had been crying since taking his first mouthful and the egg yolk that had not yet surrendered to his tongue had dripped down the side of the plate onto his shirt and tie. Only four people had ever consumed the entire gut-buster breakfast and all of them suffered from severe personality disorders. When M ordered the same again, the cafe's owner's left hand had hovered over his telephone with thoughts of calling the local Mental Health Service emergency line, but he decided that having yet another customer sectioned for eating his food would, on balance, be bad for business.

Neither Daniel's father nor his stomach actually wanted him to consume this tsunami of calories each day – this was not a diet, it was an assault – but his capacity for self-destruction outweighed his sense of self-preservation and his buttocks outweighed everything else.

It had not always been this way. As a child he had been sinuous and perpetually in motion, as much to evade his father's fists as his mother's embrace. He survived life in his parents' world where there were a hundred different words for pain. He was not inherently aggressive, yet once he discovered that he could deliver violence as arbitrarily as he received it he could not stop.

Special occasions came and went as anonymously as pigeons on a telegraph pole in a home without empathy. On his twelfth birthday, he received a jar of marmalade from his sister, a tangerine from his brother and a brief period of armistice from his parents. Jonah had beckoned him over, handed him a package and retired to a safe distance as if it were a small bomb. M reasoned that it might be, but that would have belied the true nature of their relationship. To have made his son explode would have been a tacit admission that he cared enough to disassemble him. It was the absence of caring that made his slaps sting more than the weight of their delivery.

As M tore gingerly at the wrapping paper, he had to admit that the gift was not what he had been expecting, even from a father who slammed his own head repeatedly into the wall if he got a question wrong on *University Challenge*. It was a loaded 10mm Glock hand gun.

'I want you to stop her,' said Jonah, nodding towards Bernice, who stepped backwards as if she had been headbutted.

Jonah tutted as his son held the gun by the tip of its nozzle as if it were the leg of a tarantula that was rearing up to bite him.

'I want you to stop her now.' he shouted, yet despite its volume he could barely make his voice heard. Jonah and his children stood at either end of the floral patterned settee with the curry stain on the arm, but it felt like they were a thousand miles apart on a lake of ice which was cracking beneath their feet.

Shepherding his brother and sister behind him, M placed his hands around the pistol grip and pointed the gun first at his mother and then at Jonah but he was shaking too much to aim it – it was the weight of every broken promise that had ever been made to him.

Jonah wondered why the children were not crying, but tears were just another symptom of love and they were immune to it. He had devoured them from the inside until they were empty.

'It's been a while since we went dancing, Jonah,' said Bernice, smoothing down her dress, her hands smearing a bloodied smile on the bleached white cotton. 'Dancing is the only time you look at me with joy and hold me without malice.'

'Kill her and then kill yourself,' demanded Jonah, but when he looked down at the tattered carpet he could see that the ice below his feet had broken. When the bullet hit him in the head, he plunged downwards into frozen darkness.

The image of Jonah's expression that night, like the face of his dead son, never left M. They were superimposed one upon the other, the features of each morphing and evolving. Today their eyes were the yolks of two eggs, their mouths were a Cumberland sausage and their noses were a rasher of fried bacon.

His second gut-buster breakfast only half finished, M looked into the eyes of the police constable who stood over him with the kind of disgust normally reserved for peculiarly spectacular roadkill. 'Have you finished?' asked the young officer somewhat uneasily.

Daniel's father straightened the lapels of his police sergeant's jacket with eggy fingers, put on his helmet, pushed the plate away and began the first of the fourteen stages involved in raising his audacious bulk from sitting to standing, each one ushered in with a different verbal obscenity.

'You finish it for me,' he snarled, grabbing the young officer by the scruff of the neck and smashing his face directly into the remnants of his breakfast.

For a second, just before his face hit the plate, the policeman thought he saw the face of a child staring back at him.

CHAPTER 26

Prithy Daines lived on Back Beach in Lyme Regis. Every day he would lovingly assemble and interweave the embers of the ocean into an abode, adorning it with curious shells and stones as if he were a sultan and this was his palace. Each morning he raced up and down the beach with brimming arms and fell upon a choice location perilously close to the water's edge, his fingers working in a blur of delirious erection.

When construction was complete, he would fashion a commode and a bench and the fixings for a small door, with which he would close away the world. In those moments he would stretch out his arms and touch the sides of his kingdom and in his heart he knew that this was what freedom meant. He would listen to the querulous gulls and the distant horns of fishing boats jousting for their square inch of tide and gradually, a horror would dawn upon him from which he could not escape. He was a man had who built his home in the lair of a demon who did not share and could not forgive, he was a artisan and an architect, a dreamer and a beseecher but most of all, he was an imbecile.

Every day he built his home on the beach and every day the tide would come in and destroy it. Prithy Daines hated the sea and the sea hated Prithy Daines. This was not a symbiotic relationship, more the ultimate exercise in futility, but futility was all he had. It was not that he hoped to defeat the ocean, more that one day it might tire of kicking him in the balls and pick on something its own size.

That morning he awoke at dawn to a cruel northern rain, whipping at his shrouded face with despicable vigour, a wind, bitter and revealing, chilling him to the core, and through a granular mist, where the shambles of his creation should have lain, he saw a woman in a tattered floral swimming costume.

As a rule, Prithy ignored the human race and all its vagaries, but this spur of human detritus fascinated him. He went about his daily travails, his curiosity about the woman's stoic lack of movement poking him insistently, like the finger of an elderly relative who needs the toilet. Battered by the elements, her hair was a festering mop smeared across her grey-white face, whilst her eyes remained fixed on the sea. As he worked away at his latest construction – a particularly fine plank complete with nails made a lintel, a smashed Victorian balustrade became a wall – she did not stir. He could not afford to pause, to stop was to admit defeat before it became inevitable and yet her embittered eyes drew him to her like sodden garnets.

'When will it stop?' asked the woman through a jawbone that was almost atrophied with cold.

Prithy pulled the carcass of a sack across the face of the four uneven stakes he had sunk into the ground and adorned his ceiling with a chandelier of seaweed and sea urchins. He stole a glance at the woman's toes, nails bloodied and blue, at her legs, mud-ingrained and starkly thin, at her torso, barely decent between the rips and tears in her swimming costume. He had not spoken with a human being for so long that words, when they came, felt like white-hot Alphabetti Spaghetti on his tongue.

'When will what stop?'

'The horror.'

He looked out at the sea as a burst of sunshine wove a tiny coruscating carpet which was instantly erased by the wind, at the seagulls, muzzled by the pitiless gale, at the surf, emulsifying the beach with alternating tenderness and rage. He saw it every night and every day and at last she had provided a name for it.

'I bought a train ticket to the sea but I lost it.' The woman opened her hand to evidence emptiness.

'I sat on the train and I thought, I want to change into my swimming costume but if I go to the toilet to put it on, I will lose my place. So I decided to leave all of my things on the seat, my purse and my coat and my umbrella and my bag with my sandwiches in it. I always cut the crusts off because that's the way my son likes them, the one I didn't kill.

'I looked at the man sitting beside me on the train, he had gentle hands and a lovely scarf and a cap which matched his eyes and I could see that he wouldn't mind looking after my things and I asked him and he didn't mind. So I went into the toilet and changed into my swimming costume but I couldn't remember where I had been sitting. I walked up and down the train and I was sure that it had been just beside the toilet but the man and my things had all gone. So I was fucked, completely fucked, again. I went into the toilet and had a good cry and I washed my hands again and again until the room became a paper bag that someone had just burst with their fists and I heard someone screaming my name and I recognised the voice because it was mine. So I walked up and down the train again, shouting abuse at everything and everyone and then I realised I had left my clothes in the toilet. When I went back the toilet door was locked, then I saw the man with the scarf and the hat and he was dressed in my clothes, so I picked up his wallet and I threw it out of the train window. He got angry and grabbed my arm really, really hard and the ticket collector asked me for my ticket and I told him, "of course I don't have a ticket now you tremendous fucking moron, where am I going to put a ticket, all I have left is this stupid fucking swimming costume?" And at the next station he threw me off the train and a British Transport Policeman tried to arrest me and I headbutted him and climbed over a fence with barbed wire on it and I expected him to follow me but he didn't follow me. So I had to walk to the sea in bare feet and it was miles and miles and there was a field and a cow with the face of a frosted angel and a farmer waving a gun who wore a wreath of fire and here I am a mermaid sitting on a rock.'

'And now you have found the sea,' said Prithy.

'And now I have found the sea because this is where I belong. I had a swimming lesson which I didn't enjoy because I don't like water and I don't like exercise. I floundered about for an hour, unable to swim in any direction other than down but I thought, this should be enough for the purpose of being a mermaid but then I arrived here and saw the sea and I realised it's far bigger than Kentish Town swimming baths. So I sat on this rock and looked out because that is what mermaids do and a ship came by and I wanted to lure it to its destruction but I didn't know how so I threw a stone at it but it didn't seem to notice.'

It was raining so heavily now that the raindrops were forcing Prithy down into an involuntary stoop.

'Would you like to come and sit in my...' he had never had to find a name for the structures he built, to do so would have allowed them to become visible to the waves.

'Castle,' offered the woman, walking past him and crouching down through the inadequate doorway. Prithy followed and sat down next to her on a corrugated metal sheet which he had adorned with the bodies of three dead eels and the top shell of a crab.

To say that the makeshift hut offered protection from the ardour of the storm would have been as deluded as the two minds that huddled within it, behind faces distorted with the effort of existence, but it was, at least, a different kind of discomfort. They sat, shoulders touching, each tethered so precariously to reality that one more raindrop might have cut them loose, to float off into oblivion.

'You don't look like a mermaid.'

'How many mermaids do you know?'

'One, I know one and you don't look like her.'

She studied the seaweed above her head that played with the back of her neck, at the rag doll who sat beside her, arms of shattered porcelain, eyes so sunken they echoed when he blinked. They were the eyes of her dog on the day when he died, eyes that knew more than any man what it was to exist a millisecond before existence began.

'What happens when the tide comes in? Won't this, won't we, shatter? Won't your castle be destroyed?' asked the woman.

Prithy moved his toe against hers. It felt like touching a dying plant.

'Today might be different.'

CHAPTER 27

HM Prison Belmarsh, which housed the most dangerous criminals in the UK, was renowned for its uniquely penal 'Close Supervision Centre' – a specially contained unit for inmates with dangerous and severe personality disorders. Inside this prison within a prison, the governor had recently constructed the 'Really Very Close Supervision Centre', a prison within a prison within a prison and inside this, sat Hosiah Regolith Two Swords – the psychotic axe-wielding homicidal maniac's psychotic axe wielding homicidal maniac. Every shit Two Swords shat was interrogated, every sneeze was dissected, every morsel Two Swords munched had already been masticated by the governor's hand-picked crew of elite prison commandos – his 'impenetrable wall of steel' as the governor liked to call them. 'This man,' Governor Tatty Francis told the assembled world's media, 'this treacherous, savage, wild, vicious man is going nowhere,' and nowhere was exactly where Two Swords went for the first 342 days, 12 hours and 13 seconds of his sentence.

'He's fucking escaped, how can he have fucking escaped?' squawked Governor Francis into the face of Craig Pestle, the commanding commando of the evidently penetrable wall of steel. 'Escaped where?'

'I just mean,' croaked Pestle, swallowing back the tears, 'I just mean that he isn't in his cell any more, which led me to deduce, to reach the conclusion that…'

'What about the motion detectors, what about the infrared alarms, what about the CCTV, what does the CCTV show?' yodeled Governor Francis.

'It shows…' stammered Pestle, 'it shows him being there and then him not being there and now it shows…'

'What does it show now?' shrieked Governor Francis.

'It shows him still not being there,' winced Pestle.

'What about your crack team?' howled Governor Francis. 'Seven men, who have had the finest training in the art of the observation and containment of dangerous felons that money can buy. They are supposed to have eyes on him 24–7, to track his every move, to map his every gesture, seven men who cannot be bought, who can withstand any form of physical assault, men who are unassailable, unimpeachable. What happened to them?'

'He had a migraine and had to have a bit of a lie down,' replied Pestle.

'He,' roared Governor Francis, 'what about the other six?'

'Well, Tony's on long-term sick at the moment with varicose veins, Simon has gone off prisons and is training to become a ballet dancer, the three lads from work experience didn't turn up and Terry helps his wife with their weekly big shop in Tesco on a Tuesday morning.'

Governor Francis took in this explanation as Stalin might have greeted the news that a team of NKVD officers had failed to interrogate a political dissident because they 'weren't really feeling up for it'.

'That still doesn't explain how Two Swords could have escaped from the most secure interior and exterior encasement unit in Western Europe,' retched Governor Francis. 'Has anyone been in his cell to verify this apart from you?'

'No,' sniveled Pestle, 'no one.'

'So what does that lead you to conclude, you fucking moron?' honked Governor Francis.

'It leads me to conclude that Two Swords must have surreptitiously enticed me into his cell, ripped my face off with his teeth in order to use it as a disguise and that I am in fact Hosiah Regolith Two Swords,' said Hosiah Regolith Two Swords, discarding Pestle's severed face which he had been gripping by its trailing sinews and grabbing Governor Francis by the throat.

'Oh,' snorkeled Governor Francis.

'Exactly,' said Two Swords, preparing to eat his second breakfast of the day.

*

'I don't do prison escapes, not with my back, not even if I was directly outside the prison where it was happening,' said M, from directly outside the prison where it was happening.

'Think about your career trajectory,' pleaded Inspector Thrace, 'you need to acquire some forward momentum and own the moment.'

'Don't talk to me about career trajectories you shitbaking, arselicking, cuntsandwich,' said M between spadefuls of fried egg and a ladle of coffee that was darker than the blank-eyed heart of the universe, 'I'm hardly going to make Commissioner of the Metropolitan police anytime soon. You know that I have breakfast between 9am and 11am every day, how am I going to take on enough fuel to make it through to lunch? Look at your watch you pigfucking piss-shredder, 10.55am, 5 minutes and three plates of full English to go.'

'You are, as it were, our man on the spot, M. This is your chance to save lives,' pleaded Thrace.

'Lives,' choked M, 'don't make me upchuck on my shirt you, fercockt momzer, I don't care if Two Swords himself comes in this cafe, sits down opposite me and demands my car keys, until Big Ben strikes clean-plate-o'clock in three minutes time I am not a policeman.'

M went to the toilet, gently popped his police issue radio transmitter into the piss-filled urinal and returned to his table to find Hosiah Regolith Two Swords sitting opposite him. 'Give me your car keys,' demanded Two Swords, holding out a hand branded with the hallmarks of a thousand years of quietus. M pointed at the time, Two Swords was about to speak again but M leaned over, placed his finger across Two Swords' lips and nodded at the clock again.

The two men sat in silence until the time was exactly 11am.

'No,' said M.

'I'm not a man who understands the word no,' replied Two Swords, rippling a giant pectoral in M's direction.

'Excuse me,' said M beckoning over the waitress, 'this man does not know the meaning of the word no – do you have a dictionary in this fine establishment?'

Two Swords grasped M's car keys in his grandiose mitt but his hand was quickly swallowed up by M's leather-gloved paw.

In an instant both men had grabbed the other by the throat – M's neck was the size of the average woman's waist but Two Swords' graffitied hand was up to the challenge.

'I would hate for the two of us to fall out over this after our relationship had begun so positively,' said M, who was surprised to find that his attempt to wring the life out of Two Swords' muscle-wracked neck was making not the slightest impression on his adversary's ability to breathe. It was a neck that had survived two public executions by hanging in the USA and in honesty it was partial to a bit of a squeeze. For the first time in M's life he sucked the bitter cough sweet of equality. It was not a taste he intended to become accustomed to.

'I wouldn't normally share my breakfast but given that you have been on a prison diet…' said M, letting go of Two Sword's hand, picking up a plate piled high with half eaten fried eggs and baked beans and smashing it into the side of Two Swords' head with murderous force.

'I perfectly understand and appreciate your generosity,' said Two Swords, stabbing M's car keys into the hand that had just delivered the breakfast and twisting them.

'Then you won't mind me suggesting that you add a little of this excellent home-made gentleman's relish provided gratis by this purveyor of the finest in traditional British cuisine to your already delicious petit dejeuner,' replied M, grabbing Two Swords by the hair, ramming a yellow plastic condiment dispenser up his right nostril and crushing it until projectile mustard bounced off Two Swords' frontal lobe and back down and out of his left nostril.

Two Swords wrenched his head backwards, leaving a bounteous quantity of scalp and slaughter percolating between M's fingers, and removing the double razor-bladed shank he had assembled in prison from his jacket pocket, he ran over to the table opposite and held it against the throat of a seven-year-old girl.

'As much as I was enjoying our tête-à-tête,' said Two Swords, 'it has been so very long since I have experienced the sights and sounds of old London town and I thought I might just take a little promenade in your lovely police car.' He dragged the struggling child by her arm towards the door of the cafe. 'I'm sure you are aware of how much of a butterfingers I can be with people and sharp objects, officer, we both know that at some stage this sweet little skull,' he gripped the girl's face between his fingers, 'will have to come off – beheadings are just so moreish.'

Two Swords pirouetted triumphantly and was halfway out of the door before it was closed in his face by a fully-grown Kevlar-clad walrus.

'I don't think so,' said M.

'I'm afraid I must demur,' replied Two Swords, removing the shank from the girl's neck where it left two angry tram lines across the full length of her throat and slashing it across M's Brobdingnagian stomach. When M saw the child's blood-pearled neck, he felt suddenly defective. His brain received the news that his belly had been julienned with knee-juddering uncertainty and sent him scuttering backwards.

Dragging the girl by the wrist, Two Swords exited the cafe. He forced the girl into the front seat of the police car which was parked outside, turned the key in the ignition and leaned over to tune in the radio whilst maintaining the pressure of the shank against the girl's throat.

'Nee naar nee naar nee naar – dat the sound a da poleece,' said the disembodied leather-gloved hand which had appeared from the back seat of the car and now held a penknife against Two Swords' jugular vein.

'Dear me officer, we are persistent, aren't we losing rather a lot of blood, what with having our prodigious tummy all unzipped?' rasped Two Swords.

'Stab vest, fuck pig,' replied M, 'not a scratch.'

Two Swords paused. He seemed to be luxuriating in the moment.

'We appear to have arrived at something of a Mexican standoff, officer. I intend to kill this child – it is my purpose and one I have fulfilled excellently so many times before. I fear your attempt to save her will be as dull as the blade of your little knife.'

'If you harm her it will be the end of you, piss lake,' said M, pressing the point of the knife into Two Swords' neck until blood began to pool under his skin.

'This is my calling, to divest, to dispatch, I am love, the true face of love. My victims are smitten with me, I see it in their eyes before lights out. I complete them, I fill them, I possess them. It cannot end, not with you, with something like you, not in here, like this. My end will be beauteous, it will be torrential, I will unleash an ungovernable concupiscence for violence upon the planet.'

M breathed out through his nose and watched the window blemish and clear.

'If you let her live,' said M, 'if this one child survives, you'll get another chance, you know they can't hold you – I'll fucking help you escape myself, just let this one child...'

'You can't save her, you can't save anyone, you can only destroy,' sneered Two Swords. 'To protect you have to believe, I've seen your eyes, they don't believe in anything or anyone, they have forgotten how, they have deserted you.'

Another pause but the silence was exhausting.

'Why is this child so important to you, officer? Why is saving any child important to you?'

The question. M awaited his own answer with nervous anticipation. He pointed his mouth at it and jumped.

'Because she has not been vandalised like you and I have,' replied M, 'because there are still parts of her that have not been desecrated by the stench of humanity.'

Why save this child and not his own? M asked himself as the knife teetered between his fingers. But he knew why – this was his trajectory – his father had pushed him off a snowy mountainside in a sled with no brakes. The accumulating chicanes, the sinuous masses of those whose lives M had destroyed as he careered through his sorry version of existence, did not slow him down, he doubted that even the death of his remaining son would cause his deceleration.

'Children are nothing more than grainy images – defective recordings of generations passed,' said Two Swords. 'They are ruined before they are born. Put down your knife and stop fighting.' He sensed that M was beaten, that he had finally overpowered him as he did everyone. He was magnificent, he was imperious. He turned to M and smiled, gently stroking M's hand and removing M's knife from his throat.

'You really are a verbose cuntrocket,' said M, ramming the penknife through Two Swords' jugular vein in an aurora borealis of blood.

The silence of the little girl from the front seat of the car was deafening. M tore open the passenger door and her bloodied limp body flopped into his arms. Helpless, as he had been in that hospital ward when he bore the terrible weight of his own son, he beseeched capricious life into lungs that had forgotten how to breathe.

M cried. He cried for this little girl, for the son he had lost and the one he was about to lose, he cried for the childhood he could never retrieve but although he cried, there were no tears, there was only sand.

The girl's mother was at his side, howling her name, tearing her from M's hands and as she did so, her daughter's lips parted into an enfeebled cough. The blood which covered her face belonged to Two Swords alone, her mother had been released from the hell where she had resided.

But for M, hell was boundless.

CHAPTER 28

Daniel sprinted out through the buxom gates of The Cart just as a javelin flashed past the tip of his nose and buried itself in the bonnet of a passing delivery van. School sports day was well underway and with the commencement of the field events the body count amongst pupils and teachers was already into double figures. Still breathing hard, his running vest tattooed with a Jackson Pollock, like melange of blood and vomit, Daniel stepped out into the road only to see a 1974 Austin Allegro bearing down upon him with earth-searing velocity.

'This is it then,' thought Daniel. Again.

The driver of the vehicle began braking in a way which suggested he had forgotten that servicing this 'turbo-charged deathtrap' had ceased to be a priority for a dozen or so years, leaving it unroadworthy to a degree that was almost capricious. As the little boy in the windscreen grew ever larger and his feet took root in the North London tarmac the car slewed from side to side like a crack-addicted ferret on the Cresta Run before coming to rest five millimetres from the end of Daniel's chin in a slew of rubber and brake fluid.

The passenger door swung open slowly in a manner which was intended to be intimidatory before coming off its hinges completely and falling into the road.

'Bollocks, bollocks, bollocks, bollocks, bollocks,' said M, demonstrating once again the dazzling lexicon of his vocabulary. He dislodged his guts from behind the steering wheel using the industrial wrench he stored below the driver's seat for that purpose, walked around the front of the vehicle which was currently wearing his son like a hood ornament, picked up the car door, carefully reattached it to the rotting carcass of the car and stood back to admire his work. He was truly a craftsman.

The door instantly fell off.

M was, if nothing else, an officer of the law and, demonstrating that he fully appreciated the role of the police force in society, he Frisbeed the car door into the path of an oncoming mobility scooter, peeled his son from the bonnet, deposited him in the passenger seat and drove off.

*

Daniel watched the central crash barrier of the M25 pass by with alarming briskness and proximity from the doorless passenger seat of the Austin Allegro. He mustered the remaining crumbs of faith in his father into a tiny pile and clung to the frayed seatbelt which separated him from eternity.

'Did you go to work today, Dad?' Daniel asked, hoping to calm his father down.

'Oh I worked,' M snarled. 'And I saved a little girl's life.'

Daniel stared straight ahead, slightly dazzled by the honesty in his father's voice. He felt a twinge of jealousy. 'Do you think…'

'What?' M barked.

'Do you think…you could save my life, too?' Daniel knew he was in uncharted territory.

'YOU DON'T UNDERSTAND!' bellowed M.

Silence reigned in the vehicle for a few minutes. Then Daniel noticed all the signs were facing the wrong way.

'Why are you driving this way down the motorway, Dad?' asked Daniel with practised caution.

'Since when have you become the expert on how to drive?' replied M, swerving out of the path of an onrushing articulated lorry, narrowly missing a hearse, causing a taxi to smash through the central reservation before he returned the Austin Allegro to the fast lane and accelerated to 100mph.

'I just thought that…it just seems to me…all the other cars are travelling in the opposite direction and so…'

'Fuck the other cars, Daniel,' screamed M, 'don't think like a sheep, think like a wolf.'

'A wolf who is driving the wrong way down the M25,' muttered Daniel.

M was sweating so profusely that his police tunic had adhered to him like a wet suit. He inserted an anthrax-riddled cassette of Chaka Khan's *I'm Every Woman,* and began to make the exact noise that an Alpaca makes when it is playing ladies' and gentlemen's tea parties with another Alpaca's jimmy jangles.

'Whatever you want, Whatever you need, Anything you want done, baby, I'll do it naturally,' howled M as he scooted his car around an Albanian juggernaut which had safely negotiated the 2,549.9 km trip from Tirana but now found itself doing a wheelie just outside the Clacket Lane Services before entering a drive-through McDonald's at 85mph.

'Cause I'm every woman.'

Thupp, thupp, thupp, thupp, thupp, thupp, thupp, thupp

Daniel looked up into the cruel blue sky of a world which had forgotten how to intervene, as a police helicopter hovered incredulously overhead.

'It's all in me. It's all in me, yeah!'

*

Christopher Winstanley-Stanley had an exceptionally small penis, luxuriant but wiry armpit hair which made him creak, pendulous buttocks which slapped together when he moved and a habit of ending every sentence with a dying badger-like snort. He was however peerless in the realm of quantum gravitational physics, logical positivism and all that sort of bollocks. So it was that Christopher and his tiny penis found themselves tootling out of his nasty little flat in Sevenoaks to present a lecture at Tonbridge College which he had hastily titled 'The Quantum Nature of Black Holes, Big Bang Singularity and Stuff.'

Just over fifteen minutes into his journey Christopher Winstanley-Stanley noticed what appeared to be a 1974 Austin Allegro headed in his direction at wondrous speed. He calculated that a head on collision would occur in less than 2.356 seconds unless he was able to create a series of the tiniest of quantum fluctuations which would minutely alter the course of his vehicle. 'The key is understanding the dynamics of exotic quantum matter and correlated electron systems and applying it to holographic duality,' thought Winstanley-Stanley, wobbling his steering wheel with the kind of wobbles that only a master of gravitational physics would have thought possible but which actually made absolutely fuck all difference to anything.

'Shitetoads,' screamed Christopher Winstanley-Stanley as the side of his car was hit by the police helicopter, the propellers of which had been discouraged from turning by the motorcycle that passed through them having been launched into the sky by an exploding oil tanker.

Daniel watched the carnage unfold in the rear-view mirror.

'This my childhood, Dad,' said Daniel.

'Childhood isn't a right, it's a privilege which you lost on the day you were born,' said M.

*

'This is the end of Ramsgate pier,' said M, pointing out of the window of the stationary car.

'Why?' asked Daniel, not without just cause.

'Because I intend to drive off the end of the pier and kill both of us,' replied M, without turning his head to look at his son.

'I see' said Daniel, not seeing. 'Why?'

'Why?' said M, as if this was not a question that had crossed his mind previously.

M adjusted the wing mirror so that he could see his face. He did not recognise the man who was looking back at him. He gradually released the handbrake of the car, which rolled towards the railings where a man was fishing.

'On the day I discovered your mother was pregnant,' said M, 'I read a bedtime story to Saul. In the story a little boy dreams of imitating the wings of a bird and learning how to fly. One night the boy hears a voice singing in his heart and he follows it out into space, where the stars link arms and dance to the echo of worlds. Gradually he lets go of everything that is a child until he is nothing but interstellar dust.'

Daniel looked at his father whose eyes were beaded with tears and began to move his hand towards a giant leather-gloved paw.

'And now I'm going to kill us,' said M, pulling his hand away as if he had been stung by a jellyfish.

But the car was not moving because the fisherman had leant in and put the handbrake back on.

M grabbed the fisherman by his throat. He could see the man was elderly, he knew he could have snapped his neck with a single movement but it was apparent from the fisherman's expression that he did not care.

'Time to take your little boy home,' said the fisherman.

'He's not my little boy,' said M, letting go of the old man's neck.

But his own eyes, staring back at him from his wing mirror told him that he was.

CHAPTER 29

The following morning Daniel awoke at 3.52am with a shocked inhalation of breath to find M's nose touching his own.

'We're going to the zoo, zoo, zoo, how about you, you, you, you can come too, too, too, we're going to the zoooooooooooo,' sang M, bouncing Daniel up and down on his bed with each word.

'I thought we should take a break from all of this infanticide malarky and share a little quality time, mano-a-mano. Waddya say, waddya say?'

Daniel wondered why his father didn't just pull the cushion out from behind his head and place it over his face – a delicate murder. But that was not what M needed. It seemed that he wanted to abrogate the act of his son's death, to own it but not to perform it.

'I've got us some toffee apples,' shrieked M like an excited school boy. 'We love a toffee apple, don't we?' With some effort, he peeled two sweat soaked toffee apples from the Kevlar-lined pockets of his police combat issue trousers and chomped upon them with manic gusto. All the while his eyes convulsed in ashen sockets.

Wiping toffee shrapnel from his voluptuous chops, M settled down, causing his son, who now occupied only a fraction of the bed, to draw his knees up to his chin.

'Ants,' said M, gesturing towards the speck, skittering along Daniel's skirting board. 'Did you know that ants live in little communities much like our own? They have their own political system and economy and they communicate using a very complex and ancient language which incorporates extreme violence. They live in houses which never have any more than two bedrooms and they decorate them using materials which they steal from other small creatures such as grasshoppers and diminished antelope. Although they have developed a form of medicine it is almost always fatal. Their court system is perplexing but from what we can understand they employ a draconian morality, dealing with the perpetrators of the slightest crime with cruel, swift and deadly justice. So all in all, this makes ants probably the most fascinating and sophisticated little creatures on the planet. Do you know what I think of ants, Daniel?'

Daniel didn't.

'I fucking…' M stood up and stamped down with all of his force on the ant and the skirting board, 'fucking,' stamp, 'fucking,' stamp, splintering skirting board, 'fucking,' smashed remnants destroyed under M's piston-like boot, 'fucking hate them. Now get your things on – we're going to have lots of lovely fun whether you like it or not.'

*

In the interior section of the newly refurbished enclosure in Regent's Park Zoo, Jumbe, the 300kg giant Kruger lion, sat on a rock above his pride, shook his imperious black mane, opened his immense jaws and displayed all of his thirty teeth; his serrated canine fangs for holding, puncturing and biting, his carnassial blades for shearing through flesh, his premolars, which worked like a pair of scissors, for cutting through dense physiological materials and his normal incisors that helped to scrape tissue from bones.

'It's the colour of it that puts me off,' he said, pushing the ragged lower half of a pig aside with his immense, blood encrusted paw. 'I really fancy a bowl of vichyssoise, followed by some grilled aubergine and polenta in a light garlic sauce, perhaps with a nice glass of Barbaresco Riserva from Marchesi di Gresy or a really good Monferrato Rosso for just that hint of vanilla and lemongrass.'

'I've been urging you to go for counselling for years and you can't put it off any longer,' said Malkia, the eldest female. 'You have to eat meat because you're a fucking lion. I don't want to hear one more polemic discourse about how I need to move with the times or about managing your cholesterol, it's what we were designed to do. I told you that last year when you went on the Cambridge diet and I'm telling you it again now. Eat the pig and stop trying to impress us with your knowledge of Italian wines, does anyone here look impressed, Kibibi, are you impressed?'

Kibibi stopped licking her bottom for a moment, looked confused by the question and resumed her task with gusto.

'No, exactly,' replied Malkia.

'What do you think, Imara?' asked Jumbe. 'It will be your turn to make decisions for us all next week.'

Imara, the junior member of the pride's male coalition had been chasing his tail for the past ten minutes, stopped, sniffed at a pile of fresh dung and fell asleep.

'He doesn't want to be our leader for a week, Jumbe, neither did Kibibi last week or Kibwana the week before. You cannot run this pride like an anarcho-syndicalist commune. You have to dominate us with power and violence,' said Malkia.

'Well, it just doesn't feel very democratic, that's all,' replied Jumbe.

'You are an utter head fuck, Jumbe – where does all this even come from?'

'That's a rather pejorative response, wouldn't you say, Malkia? Try to find your inner chi,' replied Jumbe. 'Now, have any of you seen my newly abridged copy of *Tess of the D'Urbervilles*? Hardy was obviously trying to make a point about the disparity in life between the rich and the poor and he does it so very well. I just know I'm going to struggle to get through again it without bringing on the waterworks.'

*

The zoo was definitively closed.

'The zoo's closed, Dad,' said Daniel, pulling his father's leather-clad hand gently back in the direction of anything else that was not a zoo.

'Stop being so negative, Daniel,' replied M, tapping on the ticket kiosk.

'It's not even five o'clock in the morning, Dad, it doesn't open until 10. It's raining and my pyjamas are getting a bit wet. Couldn't we...'

'Listen to that,' said M. There was a long period of silence. A Siberian Ibex coughed, there was what sounded like a 'shhhhhhh' and then more silence.

'You see, the animals are not closed – no, the animals are open and looking forward to meeting with Daniel and his dad and you know how I know that, Danny boy?' M asked rhetorically. 'Cos I fucking well asked them and they told me. So all we have to do is find a way of getting into the zoo so we can get this show on the road. It might have to be a bit of a naughty way but that's OK because dad's a policeman and policemen are allowed to be as naughty as they like, God said so.'

They circled the zoo until M located the staff entrance which had been secreted down a side street. The force applied when M rammed his arse against the door was 6.30×10^3kg – the same as that required to push a

61.78 kN bull elephant wearing ice skates and stranded in the middle of a frozen lake over to the shore (neglecting friction). The door did not so much open as capitulate out of extreme consternation.

They walked past the staff lockers and equipment store until M found the manager's office. The majority of the keys were in a locked display case but this was not what M was searching for. The key to the lion enclosure was on a key ring with a Colchester United key fob, hanging from a nail just under a signed photograph of David Attenborough. The rationale behind this was that no one on the planet would ever try to break into the lion enclosure on account of the fact that it contained fucking lions. M trousered it and led Daniel out of the office and into the zoo proper whilst whistling the theme tune to *Spartacus*.

*

By the time they had reached the lion enclosure Daniel had arrived at the far side of trepidation and was headed for a crash-landing between consternation and foreboding. M was pacing up and down, apparently oblivious to his son's existence. This afforded Daniel the unwanted opportunity to remind himself, from various illuminated information points, that lions are not known for their gentle good nature and compassionate dispositions. An enormous male had entered the central observation arena and appeared to be sniffing and snarling around the perimeter.

'*The lion's attack is short and powerful; they attempt to catch the victim with a fast rush and final leap.*'

'Ooh,' said Jumbe, 'a little boy. I wonder whether you might know the answer to the question that has been absolutely plaguing me over the last two weeks. I know that you conjugate "amar" in Spanish in the present tense as "nosotros amamos" but if I am using the Preterito pluscuamperfecto...'

'*The prey is usually killed by strangulation, which can cause cerebral ischemia or asphyxia (which results in hypoxemic, or "general", hypoxia).*'

The lion was staring directly at Daniel and growling angrily. Daniel backed away from the enclosure slowly, being careful not to trip, but was fixated by the lion's wicked stare. M was sitting on a bench, rocking back and forwards with his giant watermelon head in his gloved hands.

'Would it be "nosotros habiamos amado"?' asked Jumbe, 'or "nosotros amabamos"? Or is that the preterito imperfecto? Oh, I get so very confused...'

'*The prey also may be killed by the lion enclosing the animal's mouth and nostrils in its jaws (which would also result in asphyxia).*'

The lion reared up and threw its full weight at the Perspex divide. The entire side of the enclosure shook with the impact. Daniel caught his heel on a drain cover and tumbled over backwards causing one of his slippers to fall off.

'Perhaps it's "nosotros habíamos amado", or is that the preterito anterior?' pondered Jumbe. 'How does anyone ever remember? I would simply hate to be ordering a cocktail in one of those really chi-chi salons which have become so very popular on the Gran Via in Madrid, near the Jardines de Sabatini – you must know it – and find that I couldn't...'

'*Smaller prey, though, may simply be killed by a swipe of a lion's paw.*'

M rose, wiped tears from his cheeks and led Daniel to the entrance of the enclosure.

'Of course for ambience there is nothing to beat that little tapas bar just off the Calle de la Montera,' said Jumbe. 'They serve the most perfect Tortillas de Camarones but the Ceviche, well, it's out of this world, it's as if...'

'*All the lion's teeth are equipped with very sensitive nerves that allow the lion, during a bite, to find the veins and the arteries of its prey, by feeling the blood flowing inside them.*'

The lion was roaring in an excited, blood-curdling manner. Daniel had never defied his father before – one did not defy M, it would have been an exercise in futility – but as his father slipped the key into the lock of the enclosure door, Daniel tried to pull his hand in any direction other than that involving lion and lion-related environs.

'*These nerves also help the lion know when its prey is killed, because the blood stops flowing and its prey stops breathing.*'

Within seconds the door had closed with Daniel very definitely on the wrong side.

'Oh,' said Jumbe. 'I wouldn't come in here if I were you, I think there might be some lions, frightful beasts. I bought some Acqua di Selva cologne by Visconti di Modrone last week, which lends one a youthful burst of top-note freshness and one of them actually drank it, all of it and then sicked it up with a fur ball. It's this kind of decadence which led to the collapse of the Holy Roman Empire. Ohh, are you wearing pyjamas by Max and Maude, let me see, I love their intricate stitching and bold combination of silks and man-made cottons in primary colours...'

The lion appeared to be bounding towards Daniel with jaw-gaping ardour and murderous malice aforethought. Daniel tried to run but he only had one slipper and his feet would not move. When the lion was so close that Daniel could smell his wretched breath, a switch flicked on in the extrasolar region of his brain and his legs began running independently from the rest of his body. They took him into the lion's interior habitat area which appeared to offer a better option than, for example, waiting around to be torn into tiny shreds and devoured whilst still alive. His legs had not really thought through the issue of whether an enclosure containing four ravenous lions was likely to offer a small boy in pyjamas a hospitable reception but that's legs for you – the bastards.

'A Lions' jaws are short (by comparison, for example, to a wolf's jaws). They are also not capable of moving side-to-side, like the jaws of a herbivore. This helps the lion to give a steady and more effective bite, as the jaw follows a strictly vertical, scissor-like motion.'

'I think you'll find that wasn't very wise,' said Jumbe as Daniel entered his sleeping quarters. He sat down, neatly curled his tail around his feet and counted to three before Daniel's legs, thrashing like egg beaters, blurred past him, furiously pursued by Kibibi, Malkia, Imara and Kibwana.

Daniel knew he was about to die with a clarity he had not experienced when hurtling down a raging river in a sinking dinghy or hanging by his fingertips from a multi-storey car park. Death had suddenly acquired a level of inevitability and immediacy that was almost but not quite poignant. Its bitter taste filled Daniel's mouth but he would not swallow. He sprinted in several directions at once, feeling the arduous breath of the demon caress his naked heels.

'Lions are not known for their stamina – for instance, a lioness's heart makes up only 0.57 percent of her body weight (a male's is about 0.45 percent of his body weight), whereas a hyena's heart is close to one percent of its body weight. Thus, they only run fast in short bursts and need to be close to their prey before starting the attack.'

Finding himself in the furthest corner of the enclosure, twenty metre-high Perspex fencing on one side and a sheer wall of stone on the other, Daniel turned to face the beasts who had formed a heavy breathing carnivorous semicircle around him. The lions looked at each other. None of them had ever eaten live meat and the level of their excitement was tangible. Malkia chirruped in sensual anticipation and Imara and Kibwana jockeyed against each other for position but it was Kibibi who was first to attack.

'The inability of the jaw to move side-to-side is common to all cats. Lions, like all cats, do not chew their food, but swallow it in chunks. Gener-

ally speaking, the lion combines a set of big, thick and sharp teeth with an impressive bite force of 1000 pounds (1 pound = 0.453 kg).'

In the wild, it is difficult to be certain who would emerge the victor, should a rhinoceros meet a lioness in battle. Like Kruschev and Kennedy, it was the vagaries of the outcome and the prospect of both sides suffering a terrible defeat that forestalled the conflict, but it was only ever deferred.

Just as she was about to deal Daniel a first, terrible blow, Kibibi sensed, more than saw, a fully-grown male rhinoceros dressed in a metropolitan policeman's uniform with sick down the front, smash through the ranks of her pride and plough into her side with deadly finality. Her head flew into the rock face beside Daniel and her skull was cleaved in two. Her eyes still open, her steaming brains plopped onto Daniel's remaining slipper. 'Fuck this,' said M, leading Daniel by the arm and slapping aside Imara's half-hearted attempt to strike out at him, striding out of the enclosure and locking the door behind him.

*

Daniel sat with M in the car as they had sat before, as they would never sit again.

'If this is supposed to be character building,' said Daniel, 'consider my character built.'

M remained silent, his head resting on the steering wheel, his face masked with lion blood.

'Do you love me, Dad?' asked Daniel.

M looked at his son, his surviving son. 'Love died with God and table manners on the day you were born. All there is left is a dull ache that never goes away. It's in here.' He smacked his head on the steering wheel over and over again. 'It will never, ever leave me alone, you will never leave me alone until I make it happen with my own hands. I see that now.'

CHAPTER 30

Jonathan 'The Paintbrush Accident' Murray had erased his past so compre-hensively that all that could be said with any certainty was that he had been born and even this was the subject of some conjecture. Had a team of beardy, unwashed, sandal-wearing, prog rock-loving, girlfriendless arche-ologists undertaken a meticulous fingertip excavation of the billowing fronds of his psyche they would not have found the tiniest shred of empathy for his fellow man amongst the shards of clay pipes and Roman coins. There was a certain hubris about Jonathan's contempt for the human race, an alacrity with which he would seize the opportunity to throw rocks at a drowning swimmer or accidentally slam someone's balls in his car door. It was therefore no surprise that Jonathan was given the role of the D'Oily Cart's children's guidance counsellor and therapist immediately after the welcome demise of Florence Wagstaff who was mauled to death by an anteater which had become lodged in the hood of her cagoule. The very antithesis of natural causes.

The process for making an appointment with The Paintbrush was designed to be so gothically circuitous that all but a few children were discouraged from embarking upon it. Those that did were instructed to read the obituary column of the *Rochester and Chatham Daily News* where The Paintbrush occasionally left cryptic clues as to the funerals he would be attending the following week. If The Paintbrush (whose appearance was unknown to anyone) was present in the congregation and correctly iden-tified the counselling session would take place in the twenty minute gap between the end of the service and tea and biscuits.

This led to a number of unfortunate incidents.

The cremation of Mr/Ms Fernier Strunphhurr (no relation of Vassillious Strunphhurr – the inventor of the weaponised ladybird) was interrupted when seven-year-old Marcia Miller asked the widow/widower of the deceased whether she could advise her about discouraging the children in her geography class from setting fire to her head again.

The Viking burial at sea of Field Marshal Vesta Turpitude, Jnr was called to an abrupt halt when eight-year-old Marcia Miller asked the Neptune Society's Chief Operating Officer whether she would go to hell if she continued to eat the guinea pigs from the school's pet society.

*

The reconstructionist pagan mummification ceremony of Torch Nightwing Starchild was well underway when Daniel sidled into the rear of the Temple of all Galaxies which was situated between a Halal butchers and Turnpike Lane tube station. It was not difficult to identify The Paintbrush because he was dressed in a retro herringbone check suit and the remainder of the congregation were bat shit naked and smeared in blue woad and ox fat.

'Mr Murray?' asked Daniel.

The Paintbrush did not look at the child who had taken a seat next to him but his left eye flickered and closed like a failing electric light bulb.

'There is an almost lyrical quietus, an arrogance of misery in a funeral which is irresistible don't you agree Mr – '

'M, Daniel M.'

The Paintbrush jolted as if someone had just pulled a particularly thick hair out of his nostril.

'Not dead yet then, Mr M?'

'Evidently,' replied Daniel.

The Paintbrush employed the tip of his crushed velvet tie to dab at the corners of his eyes and turned to see the face of the first child who had ever tracked him down.

'So, what appears to be the problem?' he asked, smiling at his own perspicacity.

'Aside from my father trying to kill me and my mother thinking she is a mermaid?'

The Paintbrush sighed, this was exactly why his job as children's guidance counsellor was so much easier when he did not have to offer guidance to children. He had never actually met a child in the flesh and had no idea where to begin.

'Yes, well, how does that make you...' The Paintbrush shivered at the limitless frailty of the human condition, 'feel?'

'Sad,' said Daniel. 'Sad for myself. It's like I have a hole inside my stomach where happiness belongs and having nothing to fill it with. Every day is like being a spider hanging by the end of its thread in a rain storm, knowing that if it lets go it will be blown away into oblivion. Every night when I close my eyes, my mind struggles to break free and spiral down-wards towards infinity and I know that if I let it I will never be able to find my way back.'

'I see,' said The Paintbrush who had no positive childhood experiences to call upon. That was a door which had been nailed closed and bricked over. 'Perhaps you should try to interest your father in taking up a hobby.'

Daniel looked carefully into the eyes of the school counsellor. They were grey-green, like a pond in a neglected garden. There were no answers here. He stood up and left.

A wave of relief washed over the seaweed and pebbles of the barren shore of Jonathan Murray's heart but the faint aroma of a long suppressed desire to unwrite some of the damage he himself had suffered, drove his legs to stand and pursue Daniel.

*

Daniel arrived at the path that ran along the side of the New River in Islington as a swathe of cold black water parted to allow a barge to lope past towards Camden Lock. A young girl in a fairy dress sat on the bow of the boat hugging a chocolate-coloured Labrador with a lolloping tongue. This was the other world which Daniel glimpsed from time to time, a world where cataclysm did not pursue you like you were magnetised to it. He sat down on the edge of the towpath and watched mottled monochrone clouds float across the surface of the water between the ducks and detritus.

The reflection of The Paintbrush sat down beside Daniel, lowered its feet into the lipid water until its shoes and the end of its suit trousers had disap-peared. Daniel took off his trainers and socks and joined him. The tips of his toes scuffed the surface of the canal and he shivered at its icily silken touch.

'I can't remember what my mother looks like,' said Daniel. 'I try to imagine the texture of her smile, the way her eyes speak, the colour of her voice. I screw up my eyes and I punch my head and scream her name but there is nothing left. My father has burnt all her photographs and her features have been washed away like a wedding ring down a sink. She used to sit on my bed when I was younger and sometimes she would read from a journal she had written in a huge clothbound notebook with the word "fear" written on the front cover in blood but most of the time she would cry and I would hold her and stroke her hair and tell her that everything would be fine. I just want to know where her face has gone. If you can tell me that then maybe I can make sense of everything else.'

The Paintbrush took off his tie and threw it into the canal where it caught on the oar of a rowing boat before disappearing below the water like the carapace of a scarlet sea serpent.

'Sometimes I think about jumping in,' said Daniel.

'What's stopping you?' asked The Paintbrush, 'I probably would if I were you.'

'Is this therapeutic counselling?' asked Daniel, 'Because if it is, it is very subtle.'

'I don't have a clue,' said The Paintbrush. 'I live in the back of a Ford Mondeo. Last night my evening meal consisted of a bowl of cornflakes and a scotch egg. I take anti-psychotic medication which causes me to have frequent blackouts and if I don't take it I can hear my mother's and father's screams just before they died over and over again. Oh, and I am employed as a school counsellor but I detest children.'

A duck swam past so closely that its wing brushed Daniel's leg. It felt like a kiss his mother had given him on his first day of school – fleeting, disengaged.

'Part of my father loves me and wants to protect me which is really nice, it's just that a far larger part of him wants me to die.'

'So you feel abandoned by your mother and betrayed by your father?' asked The Paintbrush, getting into his stride. He was so pleased with himself he did not notice his right shoe floating off.

Daniel realised that there was something impoverished about an adult's language when they tried to describe the pain suffered by a child. They used words as if they were loaded weapons, they had lost the ability to navigate a path between the verdant groves and nuances which defined a newly formed personality, to differentiate between scars and bruises.

'My parents owe me nothing, the world owes me nothing. I get up every morning and I don't know if I am going to be given my packed lunch and taken to school or face my own death, but the ache I feel in the pit of my stomach isn't fear and it isn't hope. I can't ask my father to stop trying to kill me because he doesn't know why he started.'

The Paintbrush took a final look into Daniel's eyes, at an honesty which was unendurable.

'If a river is poisoned,' he said, 'you need to find the source.'

Without looking back he slipped into the water and began swimming in the direction of Camden Lock. His progress was inelegant – slower than the ducks and geese which quickly surrounded him, but at least it was progress.

Daniel sat and watched The Paintbrush become a punctuation mark on the ellipse of the water. He knew he had to find his grandparents.

CHAPTER 31

Daniel's grandfather Jonah shared the Hatred Cafe, in which he lived and worked, with a cat of indeterminate age and origin called The Treatment. Jonah had never liked cats, perhaps because he sensed that they alone could see through the thin veneer of his humanity into the wretched effervescing cauldron of animosity which dwelt below. When Jonah found that a cat had entered his home and was sitting in his armchair observing him with practised indifference and poorly suppressed incredulity at the human condition, he picked it up by its neck with a view to violently terminating this expression and the cat attached to it.

This was a mistake.

Jonah realised that this was a mistake because as he held The Treatment's throat between his fingers, he saw the festering contempt for all of mankind which dwelt deep within its black, black eyes; a hatred that was gothic in its intensity. What helped Jonah to concentrate on The Treatment's expression were the claws which were imbedded in his eyebrows. Jonah was attached to his eyebrows but so too, in a literal sense, was the cat. On reflection he returned The Treatment to his armchair and the cat, in turn, returned Jonah's eyebrows to his face.

It came as something of a surprise to Daniel to discover his grandfather's telephone number in his father's address book since he had been under the impression that Jonah was dead.

'Did you kill grandfather?' asked Daniel that afternoon, when it became apparent that his father had nothing planned that would be especially injurious to his health.

'Yes,' said M.

'Only I called him an hour ago and he's coming round to see me.'

M reflected for a moment, running his hand around the circumference of his catastrophic girth.

'It would appear that he's not as dead as I might have suggested.'

*

Jonah stood on M's doorstep, hopping from leg to leg, like a four-year-old in need of the toilet, in an effort to contain the internal combustion engine that dwelt between his ears.

'Boy called me, told me he had some questions needed answering,' muttered Jonah. 'Thinking of taking him to the cafe.' His flammable expression suggested that he was afflicted with a personality disorder of arrogant potency.

M had not seen his father, the familial despot who turned his childhood into a booby trapped obstacle race, since his twelfth birthday when he had almost 'funeralised' him with his own gun. To entrust his son to this savage ghost, even for an afternoon, was to be complicit in the promulgation of his wicked credo and would be an act of unprecedentedly imaginative neglect even by M's recklessly low standards.

'Be my guest,' said M. 'Get him back in time for his tea.'

*

Jonah transported Daniel to the Hatred Cafe in an aged Zephyr with plastic bench seats and a passenger door which was held on to the body of the car with gaffer tape. Every time Jonah took a corner at speed – and he took every corner at speed – Daniel slid down the bench seat towards the broken passenger door clinging to Jonah's headrest maniacally. Jonah did not believe in braking, both because he considered it to be a sign of cowardice and because the car did not technically have any brakes.

Once deposited in the apartment above the cafe, Jonah ushered Daniel to the 'dining' area – an array of random tables and chairs which would have embarrassed a school jumble sale, clustered around an ancient armchair. Daniel was transfixed as much by the pitch and yaw of the day as the way the soles of his shoes had stuck to the slick of green and orange patterned lino which covered the floor and the newspapers, scrawled with giant blood-red words, which had been stuck to the walls. He picked his way over to the armchair through the viscous half light and gingerly sat down.

The Treatment, who had been on a rare foray into the outside world to fulfil toilet-related obligations, stopped in his tracks and stared at Daniel in disbelief.

'Get out of the armchair now,' said Jonah so loudly that it made Daniel shrink back into it.

A bead of sweat had trickled down between the eyes of The Treatment, along the rift valley of scars that traversed his nose and on to his chin where it hung like a flawed diamond before plopping onto the floor. His eyes were visceral pools, every sinew tensed to strike.

It took fully ten minutes to unpick the claws of The Treatment one by one from Daniel's chest and all the while the cat emitted a low, almost imperceptible growl.

'That will teach you to sit in another man's chair,' said Jonah.

*

Jonah settled down at the least precarious of the tables in the cafe and beckoned Daniel over to join him. In the semi darkness, Jonah's face gained an ethereal quality reminiscent of a slightly mouldy Halloween pumpkin. He lit up a cigarillo, inhaled so deeply that his lips subsided completely into his face and leant forwards until his nose was almost touching Daniel's.

'What you wanna know?' His question floated in a fug of cigar smoke.

'Why is my father trying to kill me?'

'That's a weak question, boy. Why you asking it? My son wants to kill you he got his reasons. You want to stop him then stop asking old men what to do and take an axe to his head while he sleeping.'

'Your son is trying to kill your grandson and that's your advice?'

'What you bleating about, boy? Count yourself lucky my son's no good at killing. Tried to execute me when he wasn't much older than you are now, bullet went in the side of my skull here,' he pointed at a thumb-sized indentation on the side of his forehead, 'came out here,' he grabbed Daniel's hand and held it against a giant crater in the base of his skull. 'Took out a piece of my brain the size of a golf ball. Looks like you not dead either so he ain't got no better at it. Now when I kill a man he stays killed.' His grip on Daniel's hand tightened and with their increased proximity it became apparent that his grandfather was somewhat unfamiliar with the concept of personal hygiene. 'Murdered my first man with an ironing board because he looked at your grandmother the wrong way in a bar.'

'Why?' asked Daniel.

'My father told me, never trust a man who cannot find violence in his hands. When I made mistakes he corrected me with his fists. Man starts an argument with you, you finish it, man does you wrong, you finish him.'

'What about forgiveness?'

'Don't use words you don't understand.'

'But I don't want to be like you and I don't think my father does, not really. There must be another way.'

'Time was, I ask my father that same question. I was sixteen years old and he had just come out of prison. He put on a mask, enough to make them believe he wasn't broken inside but we knew different. It wasn't a mistake they made again. My mother spilled whisky on his shirt day after he got home and he went to put his fury onto her again but I stood in his way. When he went inside I had been no higher than his waist but now I was taller than him, thought I was something special. Hit him square in the face with my best shot and he didn't blink. Took me out to the garden by my hair and threw me into the mud. Asked him to forgive me then, as my nose and mouth fill up with dirt but he just laughed. He only laugh when he was hurting people who loved him. So don't you talk 'bout forgiveness. I don't blame your father for taking out the best part of my brain and you shouldn't blame him for tryin' to kill you if that's what he has to do. It's in our blood, no hiding from it. You either got to stop him or you gonna die.'

Jonah let go of Daniel's hand and his face receded into the filthy gloaming.

Daniel could not allow himself to believe that all the future held for him was a daily cage fight with a demented bull elephant.

'Do you think that grandma might be able to…'

Jonah sat bolt upright, he seized Daniel's arm, stood up and wrenched him towards the door.

'Enough questions. Taking you back. I got nothing else for you.'

'But if I could just speak with her then…'

Jonah stopped and knelt down until his mouth was against Daniel's ear.

'Sometimes the crocodile kills because she need to and sometimes she kill because the act is so full of grace she just has to feel it again. Finding her might give you another answer but I don't think it's going to be one you want to hear.'

CHAPTER 32

School – that joyful daily sprint between classes while slightly gentler and more amicable punches rained down upon him from his new friend Dorsal Grellman – was Daniel's only respite. His conversation with his grandfather had convinced him that as much as he still loved his father, a return home would almost certainly lead to yet another convoluted attempt to terminate his existence. Sleeping standing up in his school locker was a wholly more attractive option.

It had been three long days and nights, by which time Daniel had developed back pains better suited to an octogenarian, when an envelope was nailed to Daniel's desk at the end of the school day. In it was a card that had more in common with a ransom demand from a psychotic kidnapper than an eighth birthday party invitation. He was offered the option of non-attendance but was left in no doubt that this would be yet another decision that would shuffle him off this mortal coil.

It sounded better than going home. Or waiting around in the boys' bathroom until the janitors left for the night and he could slip back into his locker. Besides, Ferris had also received an invitation – though his had been superglued to his forehead.

*

Dorsal's home nestled between a toxic waste disposal unit and a multi-storey processing plant which turned bird beaks and arthropods into meat products for the fast food industry. It was a somewhat symbiotic relationship; on more than one occasion a lorry load had been delivered to one rather than the other in error and thus far, no one had complained. The stench of the worst excesses of humanity had intertwined with Dorsal's aunt on a subatomic level and she knew that her final years would be spent staring from her kitchen window at a mountain of beaks and exoskeletons glinting in the setting sun.

Daniel and Ferris were ushered into Dorsal's house by a woman of such dazzling decrepitude, it seemed unlikely she would see out the rest of the day. It was difficult to know whether she had been expecting them; she was unable to muster words of any kind and after showing them into what was more of a crypt than a room, she collapsed into an armchair and fell into a deep sleep. It occurred to Daniel as he squinted into the dank sepulchral darkness at what appeared to be a mantelpiece decorated with animal skulls that Dorsal's birthday party was unlikely to feature any aspects of the word 'fun' even in its broadest sense.

Parting the gloom as if carving a knife through chocolate fondant, Daniel discerned a stubbornly enormous figure sitting cross-legged on the floor on the far side of the room.

'I hope you weren't expecting trifle and pass the parcel,' said Dorsal.

'I don't know what we were expecting – at best, not to die in excruciating pain,' suggested Daniel.

He sensed more than saw that Dorsal was standing – it was a subtle and liquid movement for something so large. When a rabid dog enters a passage of stillness all that one can say for certain is that it will be short-lived. Daniel flinched in readiness for the first blow.

'I understand your father is trying to kill you,' said Dorsal. 'The head teacher told me over a glass of Chianti in his office last week.'

'I didn't think he believed me,' said Daniel

'Oh, he believes you, he just doesn't care. He said that it would be one less child between him and his retirement. He just asked your father not to do it on school premises.'

'He's spoken to my father about this?'

'At open day, between Geography and History, he has ten minute slots for parents who want to murder their children. It's more common than you might imagine.'

Dorsal was looming over Ferris and Daniel, his breath was fetid. He reached out and placed his hand on Daniel's arm, it was the first time he had done so without trying to pull it out of its socket.

'We could kill him – kill your father.' Dorsal's lips parted into a death skull grimace. It took a while before Daniel realised that this was a smile.

'I don't want to kill him, he loves me, if he didn't he wouldn't keep trying to murder me.'

Dorsal took a step backwards, the word 'love' accosted him. It was as if Daniel had landed a blow in the middle of his forehead.

Realising suddenly that he was going to be sick, Daniel struggled out of what appeared to be the only room on the ground floor of the house, up an uncarpeted stairway shrouded in blue-black dusk and into the first door he came too. Daniel's bilious senses were assaulted by the contrast with the rest of the house. The room appeared to have been bleached white; the walls were covered by huge, dexterously graphic paintings of wild animals, real and imagined, slaughtering prey; there was a mantelpiece besieged by framed photographs and on the floor was a mattress covered by a single sheet. Daniel recognised the child in the photographs – there could have been very few other three-year-olds who were the size of a fully-grown man. It struck him that the faces of the couple draped around the infant Dorsal resembled the snapshots of murder victims that were printed in newspapers – there was some intrinsic part of humanity that had been lost from their expressions.

'They used to be my parents,' said Dorsal.

Daniel assumed that if he turned around, his skull would join the others on the downstairs mantelpiece.

'When they see me it reminds them what they really are, so they don't see me any more.'

'Did you paint these?' Daniel shrugged towards the artwork on the wall hoping that this would not provoke an onslaught.

Dorsal spun Daniel around and picked him up by his shirt collar until their faces were level.

'If you tell anyone about this room I will really fuck you up.'

'You're going to fuck us up anyway, aren't you?' wheezed Daniel.

'You are my friends now, so yes, I am still going to fuck you up, I just won't enjoy doing it quite as much. But if you tell anyone about what's in this room, I will rip apart your ribs and I will eat your heart whilst it's still beating.'

This was not an image that appealed to Daniel.

Dorsal put Daniel down and straightened his shirt.

The door opened and Ferris entered holding a Kermit the Frog birthday cake with six candles. He was wearing a party hat which had been stapled to his head and his fingers appeared to have been baked into the cake. Two more candles had been stuffed into his ears and their flames licked at his sideburns. Ferris was smiling as ever – he had never been invited to a birthday party before and had no way of knowing that this was not standard practice.

'Are you just going to let your father kill you, Daniel?'

Dorsal's question glistened like the dazzling seeds of a sparkler – Daniel had reached out to touch these words in the void many times before but his fingers had always been seared.

'My grandmother has a rather unhealthy degree of insight into the mind of a murderer – I thought I could ask her advice,' replied Daniel. 'She lives on a mountain in Milton Keynes. I asked my grandfather for directions and he told me to come out of the station, turn left at the organic greengrocers and follow the screams of the damned up to the vale of tears.'

'We're going to struggle to find that on a sat nav,' said Ferris whose hair was, essentially, on fire.

'He also told me she was one of the most dangerous people on earth,' said Daniel.

'Milton Keynes it is then. I'll tell the headmaster to close the school tomorrow so you won't miss any lessons and we can get an early start. You can pay the train fare, Ferris, you little bastard,' said Dorsal, picking Ferris up and carrying him over to the toilet where he rammed his head repeatedly into the brimming urinal.

It was the best day of Ferris' life.

CHAPTER 33

PC David Daindridge stared out of the police car at a world from which he was separated by the width of a car window on one side and thirty-two stone of bastard on the other. Sergeant M was relating one of his horrifying anecdotes, punctuating each of the myriad of obscenities with a sharp poke in the young officer's ribcage. There was more anger than there usually was – though Daindridge remained blissfully unaware of this – due to Daniel's fortuitous escape from the jaws of death the night before. Had he come home on schedule, and opened his bedroom door, a jerry-rigged crossbow would have solved M's problems once and for all. But it was not to be so.

It was more an assault than a conversation and Daindridge found himself wondering, as he often did, just how painful it would be to sprint into the waves of the winter sea and never stop. 'Every single day for six months I walked past a man in a set of threadbare fatigues on my way to work,' said M. 'Explosion of white hair, reeking of piss, carrying a canvas ruck sack. I would get to the chemist on the high street just as he was coming out of The Crescent and he would always have the biggest smile on his face, the kind that makes you want to punch it away. This particular morning, my wife came into the kitchen where I was preparing my usual pre-breakfast snack of twelve rashers of bacon and a king-size black pudding, picked up the frying pan with which I was preparing said feast, shouted "enjoy your breakfast you, fat fuck" and smashed it into my face with such force that I fell off my chair onto the floor and shat myself. It was one of those moments which really make you question where all the romance in your relationship has gone.

'So, rather than walk up Haverstock Hill to Hampstead Police station, I decided, on balance, given that my cheekbone had been shattered and the word "Teflon" had been burnt in reverse onto my forehead, that I had better pop in to A & E.

'Just at the bottom of Hampstead Heath I saw the white-haired man with the canvas ruck sack darting off into a bush and despite the obvious inconvenience of having only half a face, my police instincts kicked in and I decided to follow him. When he reached this small area of dense undergrowth, he crawled inside, singing "Flash, ah ah, saviour of the universe, Flash, ah ah, saved every one of us," in a discordant falsetto, took something out of his bag, buried it and left. I managed to scramble in with no little difficulty and discovered, inside a plastic zip lock bag, a small red velvet gift box, tied with a silk bow and inside that a nose, lovingly severed from its owner, not a trace of blood. I dug out thirty bags, all containing human noses and do you know what I did, Dangerous Dave?' Each word was punctuated by another painful prod in the ribs.

Daindridge drank in the world through the distorting facets of a raindrop as it bled down the passenger window of the car in pursuit of oblivion. How much pain would he feel if he was hit by a train? Would there be a moment of such revelatory agony that his mind would become a perpetual bedlam, or would it just be a full stop at the end of the incoherent sentence that his life had become?

'I buried all the boxes exactly where I found them and got up ten minutes later every day so I would never see the murderous old twat again and do you know why? The paperwork, can you imagine the shitting paperwork? Thirty fucking noses. Fuck me. No thanks.'

The tributaries of a dozen raindrop rivers traversed the car's passenger window, allowing Daindridge to view North London through a bleeding spectrum of convergent colours. He watched a disembodied man in a green balaclava, the sleeves of his red and black leather jacket melting down and around his sawn-off shotgun as he entered NatWest Bank in Haverstock Hill.

'Errrrr...' Daindridge sat bolt upright, pointing at the door of the bank.

Sergeant M crammed the last of the twelve doughnuts he had joylessly consumed into his mouth and tutted.

'Sir, I think...'

'You're not here to think, Dangerous Dave, you're here to drive, listen to my diabolical anecdotes and shut the fuck up.'

'There's a bank robbery happening.'

Sergeant M had been pouring fossilised sugar fragments from the upturned empty doughnut bag into his gaping mouth and as he turned, the sugar spilt down his uniform and into his ample lap. He was not best pleased.

'There's a bank robbery happening where?'

'In the bank, Sir.'

'Oh for fuck's sake,' grunted Sergeant M, commencing the arduous process of convincing his momentous arse to accept the pleading missives it was receiving from his brain seriously and move.

'Shouldn't we call this in?' asked Daindridge, who wanted to cry, urinate, vomit and scream at the same time and would have done so had he been left to his own devices. He picked up the car radio but a leather-gloved trotter encased his wrist and forced him to drop it.

'If we call it in, it's a KN33(22), a LN43 and two N9.3s. If we deal with it ourselves it's a G41 and I can be sitting at home tonight curled up in front of the football with two plates of curry and a pizza.' This was a less than persuasive argument but Daindridge knew that Sergeant M was far more dangerous than a man with a shotgun and he plunged unenthusiastically into the North London deluge.

As they entered the bank, the man in the balaclava was standing on the chest of the prone security guard and had already blown a hole through the ceiling and the bank manager's left arm. He turned to see what appeared to be a hippopotamus in a police uniform bearing down on him. The hippopotamus was not moving quickly but as anyone facing an impending impact with such a beast will testify, that does not really matter. He tried to reload the sawn-off, realised he had not brought any more cartridges, swung the shotgun at the creature and then the world became a black velvet coffin.

As he lay amongst the remnants of the bank robber, Sergeant M felt the barrel of a low calibre pistol press against the side of his face. It probably should have occurred to him that there would be two bank robbers but his reasoning was as coherent as a portrait defaced by acid and the only mystery the world still held for him was that Marks & Spencer continued to manufacture pants large enough to accommodate his ever inflating buttocks.

CHAPTER 34

'Get up slowly and make your way into the safety deposit box room,' growled the thief, his voice a melange of contempt and desperation suffused with ferocious anger. The gun pressed harder against M's cheekbone.

'Can you imagine me getting up anything but slowly?' Sergeant M struggled to find purchase until Daindridge helped him to his feet.

The safety deposit box room was the size of a large toilet and as the bank robber closed the door behind him M felt the walls and ceiling close in, as if he were a wilting flower, pressed between two slices of wood by an avaricious child. They were motioned to sit down on the floor beside a small table. The electrical spaghetti of the dismembered CCTV hung from the wall and the contents of the safety deposit boxes had been piled onto the table where Robber 2 now sat.

'When I pull this trigger,' the robber leaned down and pushed the gun into Daindridge's eye socket, 'your brains will explode and even people who know you, who love you, won't recognise you, they won't even be able to look at you without vomiting.'

'That's pretty much the story already,' said M, who could feel sweat pooling between the layers of his voluminous lard. 'Anyway, a bullet from a little gun like that would just blow a hole through his eye socket and out through the back of his head. A glass eye and a bit of wadding stuffed into his brain cavity and he'd look better than he does now.'

The robber's features were hidden behind his balaclava but his eyes were eloquent in their bitter antipathy for M.

'How do they allow a rancorous fucking animal like you to become a policeman? You're grotesque, like the kind of bloated, fly-infested buffalo that wallows in its own shit in the far corner of the worst kind of zoo. You are fucking disgusting – how does a human being let itself get in to this kind of state?'

M wasn't listening – the contorted mouth, framed in green patterned wool, had become a huge glistening maggot, writhing on a hook.

'When my son died,' said M, 'when I heard that he had died, I waited at the hospital for his body to arrive. They show you into a room, a room about the size of this one and there is an empty bed for dead sons and an empty chair for doctors whose words defile you, who touch your shoulder like a cannibal because you are so much edible flesh to them. When they arrived with my boy, his little body, swaddled as if he was being lifted out of his bath, I became invisible, because he was the best of me, he was all of me of any substance in this vile, shit-infested world. What was left, what was left in that room, in this room, is raw sewage. So shoot me, you execrable little pissant, shoot me in my guts where it is going to hurt the most and do it now before I rip you apart with my fucking teeth.'

Placing his hands on Daindridge's shoulder and the robber's knee, he levered himself up with surprising grace and punched the man in the face with such force that for a moment it seemed that his head might depart from his shoulders. He plucked the gun from a hand which was still clenching and unclenching and it was at that point he noticed the blood rose, blossoming on his shirt.

'You've been shot,' Daindridge reached out a timorous finger and touched the hot red petals.

M pulled open his shirt and traced his fingers around and into the entry wound in the pregnant mound of his gut. A small calibre handgun, fired at close range into thirty-two stone of blubber and kebab – if he still had any vital organs in there, this pea shooter wouldn't have found them.

'I need this gun, David,' said M, 'I need it to bring an end to the relentless horror, I need to use it to kill and I can't be stopped. You'd stop me, wouldn't you, David? You'd have to stop me, it's what people like you do, put your finger in the dam of bestiality.'

'I…' Daindridge's vocabulary lay on the floor around his feet, he scrabbled around for words like 'life' and 'mercy' but they were lost amongst the dust bunnies and crevices. All he could find was 'please,' which, as he uttered it became an entreaty to do what he most feared yet most desired.

M raised the gun and shot Daindridge at close range directly between the eyes. The young man's mouth formed into an O as he eased slowly backwards as if in slumber. Automatically M reviewed the crime scene. There would be no one to gainsay the order of events, villain shoots young copper and fat copper, fat copper bravely snaps villain's neck. Murder weapon and fat copper missing but that was just a footnote – it would read well, the brass would like it and reality, as ever, would slide off the page.

He had tried and failed to slay his own son and now he had killed someone else's. He wanted to care, for it to hurt more than the bullet in his stomach, but honestly – he had felt neither. His life was like a pool of quicksand and he had been drowning in it slowly for years. The only question now was who he took down with him.

CHAPTER 35

After two rays of building castles in the waves only to see them gutted and consumed by a gluttonous ocean, Daniel's mother had earned, if not Prithy's trust, then a dilution of his contempt.

They were staggering, heads bent, alone on the beach in the early hours. Ice had formed into shallow opaque pools between the drifts of sand and as they broke it with their blistered feet they could see their faces shatter in a way that meant they could never be reassembled.

'There is a garden in which I sit when the cold has me by the throat,' said Prithy. 'It is the place where I first realised I could defeat the sea, that it could be defeated, if one understands its purpose. The mermaid lives there – I could show you it.'

Daniel's mother could neither defy nor consent, her feet followed Prithy's and that was all that life consisted of now. They arrived at a line of beach huts, their bright paint corroded into peeling leather rivulets by the talons of a force that would return them to their elemental form. Prithy ducked down into a shallow trench, up into the stomach of a sky blue shack through an unlocked service flap and she followed. She emerged into a tangled thicket of ivy and bindweed to find Prithy tearing at the green brown veins, unearthing a bench seat, a coal burning stove and some matches. The fire filled her with a warmth so intense that she wanted to inhale it so that it resided in her lungs. Something inside her, where so much was broken already, snapped and she began to weep for the life that continued just beyond her grasp, as if she were Tantalus and her family was the fruit.

'Whenever I wanted to take my dog for a walk it would hide,' she said. 'I just had to stand up and look for its lead and it would crawl under a bed or behind the settee, sometimes into spaces so small that it must have hurt itself to get in to them, anything but walk with me. On one occasion it wedged itself behind the fridge and I had to lever it out with a plank. Our dog had no name so we could never call it. We developed a complex series of hand gestures and whistles which, since neither we nor the dog understood them, made communication an ultimately unsatisfactory process. I forgot exactly what a dog was for, shortly after he arrived, by then the world was like two jigsaw puzzles that had been jumbled up together; but when I tried to use the dog as an ironing board it bit me with such unbridled fury that I still have a fragment of its tooth embedded in my knuckle.

'This particular Friday, Daniel was off school because of the snow and I found the dog cowering under a pile of frozen leaves and branches in the back garden. The dog had assumed the same expression as Daniel did when I tried to rationalise with him – a mixture of unexpurgated contempt and fear. It knew, they all knew, that I was like a wounded alligator floating on the surface of a river, directionless, floundering, but still capable of one last terrible attack. I dragged the dog out – I think it knew it would perish in that garden if it wasn't discovered but it had accepted that – and down the road to the Heath. I had no idea if I had taken it for a walk already that day, I had no idea what taking it for a walk consisted of but I was going to do it anyway.

'Middle Lake on the Heath is a landmark for migrating birds because of its size and normally it's busy with children feeding the ducks and swans, but it wasn't busy that day. That could be because it was minus four and it could be because I was screaming so loudly and the dog was moaning like a child begging for time itself to come to an end. I left the dog tied to a bench and walked out on to the ice – right into the middle of the lake. I got down onto my hands and knees and saw, in my reflection, exactly what they all saw, the children, the dog, the fucking milkman who still delivered even though I threw his bottles back at him – it was the void and it was in my eyes and it was labyrinthine. I took off my shoe and I hammered with the heel at that reflection, I hoped that beneath it I might discover the cobwebbed shards of my dignity. The ice begged me to stop as I hacked away at its pristine layers, my arm arced and fell and the dog struggled until its collar bit into its throat – it was like the dance of a murderer.

'Eventually the face below my fists floated apart and the dull black velvet of the water below embraced me like a disciple, kissing my body until it was extinguished. Then the dog was upon me, pulling me back to the surface, its throat was wrecked from where it had broken free but it kept on coming and coming with its teeth, struggling against the ice, its feet splaying and skittering. Somehow, eventually, it dragged my body from the water onto the snow-matted soil.

'I fucking hated that dog and it hated me. I would love to tell you that I lay on the bank of the lake and held it in my arms, sharing its warmth, discovering some hitherto untapped love for the species canine, but I can't. It had saved my life, I knew it had killed itself in the process and that really pissed me off. It waited to see whether I was still breathing and when it could see that I was, it sunk its teeth into my left thigh and that's how it died, inflicting as much pain as it possibly could.'

Sarcastic applause spewed from deep within the foliage at the rear of the hut and a woman emerged clothed in seaweed strung with decaying seagull heads. Her hair appeared to have been recently excreted onto her head and her skin was befouled leather and rope. She waved a hand, depraved by arthritis. 'I thought that Prithy was the most stultifyingly depressing little shitebag that had ever washed up on this beach but apparently I was wrong. This really is a seminal moment.'

'I am a mermaid – I am here by serendipity,' croaked Daniel's mother.

'You are a middle-aged woman in a torn swimsuit following around a maniac who lives on the beach in a pile of twigs and bird droppings.'

'This is my little piece of England and I must defend it from the warrior Neptune,' protested Prithy.

'Exactly – he's a headcase and you are lost.' The woman lowered herself with no little effort onto the bench in front of the fire, beside Daniel's mother.

'This is perdition,' bellowed Prithy.

'This is Lyme Regis,' the woman replied, 'go and build some more sand-castles on the beach.'

Prithy was about to protest but the woman dismissed him with a disparaging flick of the wrist.

Daniel's mother had nothing more to offer. She felt herself plummeting into the nether reaches of her psyche and plunged her face into an endless pool of tears. She had seen this place in sidelong glances during the worst of her waking dreams and knew that if she drank from this pool there would be no returning. The woman grasped her chin with fingers of petri-fied bone, turned her head gently so that it was inches from her own and after stroking the straggles of sand and mud from her face, headbutted her with tremendous force. Daniel's mother collapsed to the floor of the hut and the woman fell upon her until the solidified strands of her hair trailed into Daniel's mother's eyes and mouth like rats' claws.

'You selfish, selfish bitch. How dare you come here and abandon your son.'

Daniel's mother spat out two shattered teeth as she tried to speak.

'I killed my son,' she said, 'I have lived on the margins of sanity for years, spare me your fucking contempt, you can't know what this has made me, made of me.'

The woman grabbed her by the ears, spittle drizzling between an abandoned graveyard of teeth.

'I am the old woman with the supermarket trolley and two hundred brimming carrier bags, yet I have never been into a shop, I am the face that you look at a second time for the incandescent horror of it, I am the stubborn stain that this country scrubs and scrubs at but cannot remove. I have never been kissed, never felt a man's hand other than in rage and I would give my eyes just to have known how it felt to hold my own child in my arms. This is the life of a mermaid, it is my life and it is wretched and it is interminable. Now fuck off back to where you came from and prove you can still be a mother to your son.'

CHAPTER 36

Chasney Mint had worked as an mortician in Milton Keynes for more than forty years. It was not so much a calling, more a self-fulfilling prophecy.

Born in 1930 in Paris, his parents found themselves in exactly the wrong place at exactly the wrong time when their neighbours decided to pop round for a holiday bringing 2,750 tanks and 2,315 aircraft with them. When his family was invited to spend some time in Poland – a country they had never previously visited – he had survived by dint of his mother's Catholic lineage and his body's apparent inability to die. His father, uncles and aunts, everyone he knew and loved had been considerably less fortunate. The cross in their lounge, the star on his father's and uncle's jackets had been shapes and colours no more significant to him than the jagged lines in a broken mirror, but to others they were determinative of whether they remained in their homes or they all fell down.

Chas wondered at night, whilst others engaged in cotton wool somnambulism, whether he should have been a man, a mensch, and insisted upon the star and not the cross; whether he should have taken his father's hand and not let go when his mother told him to say goodbye in a way she had never done before. Should he have stood shoulder to shoulder with his school friends when the stones flew, friends who had laughed but had forgotten laughter, whose cries stained walls that were now and would forever be monuments to unimaginable excess? What was survival?

Yet he endured the camp, he had children who were born from this terrible game of chance and they were Mints and not Mintovskis' as his father had been, children with strong bones, thick hair and unwavering smiles. He had given them a strength that was not his to bestow – it was the strength of those who he had lost, whose faces and voices he could no longer remember. It was their legacy and he was no more than a cipher.

Whilst Chas had spent more than four decades as an embalmer that is not to say that he was good at his work – he was certainly not. He had established three 'looks' regardless of gender, age or ethnicity and he stubbornly bestowed these without demur.

Look 1: Gloria Swanson – the ageing Hollywood harlot;

Look 2: Bela Lugosi – the vampire;

Look 3 (and by far the most objectionable): Giuseppe the clown.

It would seem, even looking beyond the superficial, that Chasney Mint was set to self-destruct and yet within the community, his community, there had arisen a sense of appreciation, that these were no longer just the faces of their beloved but the faces of others, whose lives had been stolen from them. They understood that to Chasney, these extinct faces were like the screams of the defiled, whose queue he should have joined, in whose arms he should have died. They were a love poem which had taken more than sixty years to write and to which his patrons were proud to add their stanza.

Reaching over for some more rouge, Chas realised that he was not alone in the mortuary. In the doorway stood two children and something that looked as though it might have been a child, had it not been over six feet tall with the body of a gorilla.

'We were hoping you might be able to help,' said Daniel, 'we came out of Milton Keynes station, turned left at the organic greengrocers…'

'I would have said,' interrupted Ferris, 'that it was more of a holistic retailer with produce that varied between locally grown root vegetables and other edible tree-based items, such as…'

Chas noted that the small child with two pairs of glasses and Holbeinesque acne had begun to speak but had been interrupted by the gorilla throwing him to the floor and standing on his face.

'But when we asked people where we could find the screams of the damned and the vale of tears they directed us to you,' said Daniel.

Silence passed between them like the reaction to a wedding invitation sent to an ex-girlfriend. Is this what people really thought of him, of his work? Chas examined the children's expressions, it was as if their innocence had not simply been lost but replaced by betrayal.

'What are you doing to that man's face?' asked Daniel with eyes that looked one hundred years old. Chas had seen eyes like this before; it was not a happy memory.

'I am preparing him for his loved ones.'

'He looks like an evil clown – are you sure that his family will like it?' asked Daniel.

Chas looked, really looked at the face he was besmirching. He had never had any complaints but he did gain the sense, in whispered glances, in the shuffle-footed dance of the recently bereaved, that there was much they were not saying.

'I don't really know. Perhaps this isn't about those who have been left behind and what they feel. What are you three doing here, what can I possibly do for you that others can't?'

'We are looking for a mountain. The mountain my grandmother lives on,' said Daniel.

'Here, in Milton Keynes, a mountain?'

The boys seemed to tense, they must have known that the answer to this question was inevitable. Chas sensed that there was no capacity left in these children for any more rejection. He could not unwind the fates of the friends and family he had left behind, but perhaps here was a chance, possibly his last chance to justify his solitary survival.

'You know, there might be a mountain here,' he said, 'it's just that I have never looked at it in that way.'

CHAPTER 37

It had stopped snowing for the first time in several days and the boys trailed a staccato centipede of footprints behind those of Chas, as he stop-start-rested his way through the middle of the old village of Milton Keynes.

Chas paused outside the Swan Inn. 'You see this tree,' he gestured at a singularly vacant patch of earth devoid of anything remotely tree-like. 'It was said that when this ancient elm died, no more male children would be born in the village.'

Dorsal wondered whether he could punch Chas hard enough to cause him tremendous pain without actually killing him. Appraising his potential victim, Dorsal concluded that since Chas's skin appeared to have been constructed from strips of tissue paper which had been poorly stuck together, anything more than a gentle pat on the back would have eviscerated him. He decided to try looming – it usually initiated a desire for compliance.

'Is this the way to the mountain?' Dorsal stood over Chas, grimacing in a manner which would have intimidated a medium-sized Bengal tiger, but Chas had been taken to the brink of death by an enemy which did not countenance the continued existence of his species. This child, albeit a child which appeared to be about to dismantle him as if he were an unwanted Airfix model, could not scare him – he no longer had the capacity for fear.

Chas cleared the snow off a bench which had been positioned for people to admire the now ex-tree and sat down with an exultant groan, his little legs swinging back and forth. 'Why is this mountain so important to you?' he asked.

'My grandmother lives on the mountain – we were hoping she could offer some advice about my father's problem.'

Daniel sat down on the bench besides Chas and began swinging his legs in time with the old man and they were soon joined by Ferris. 'For fuck's sake,' Dorsal hissed, joining them whilst at the same time hoping that someone truly homicidal would not come by at that very moment and witness him letting the side down.

'And what is your father's problem?'

'My failure to die.'

Chas stopped swinging his legs and looked at Daniel as if he had not seen him before. He had been a victim of truth in its every guise, it had crept up in the night and held a knife against his throat, held his head under water, beaten him until he could have reached out and shook death by the hand, he knew truth and this boy was glutted with it.

He roused his joints into movement against a chorus of protests. Every time he sat down he feared he might not have the willpower to stand again, yet willpower defined him. He would always stand and he would always move forwards putting distance between himself and the atrocities of the past.

'Is your grandmother someone with insight?'

'My grandmother made my father, helped make my father what he is – I hoped she might be able to suggest a way to stop him.'

'She killed Batman with her bare hands,' barked Ferris excitedly, 'and pushed Darth Vader off Beachy Head.'

'She understands death,' added Dorsal.

Chas began walking back towards the town centre, trailed by a phalanx of troubled youth. 'I understand death too,' he said, 'it's where I grew up.'

Dorsal caught up with Chas, his prodigious footprints devouring those of the old man as if they were plankton. He could have burst him there and then in the snow, like a used paper bag and yet he felt the urge to trust him. Trust did not sit well with Dorsal, he had given it freely to adults and it had earned him abandonment, left him beleaguered, hunched against the ravages of childhood with anger his only refuge. He hungered for destruction, to destroy, it mattered not what or whom and it had already been too long.

They arrived on the outskirts of the town, fists of bitter cold pressing hard against their chests, old and young. An unfashionable district, in a delinquent city, in a country which could neither be shaken, nor stirred. Chas paused outside a butcher's shop which clung desperately to the husks of neighbouring buildings long since divested of their occupants. As he began to enter, Dorsal grabbed his upper arm. 'This is no mountain.'

'I am in no position to ask you to believe in me or any adult,' Chas unpicked Dorsal's hand finger by finger, 'just indulge me for a few more seconds.'

The shop was an Armageddon of severed limbs, blood-spattered walls and sordid weaponry; its proprietor, a slight man with disproportionately huge hands, froze, with what appeared to be a cutlass raised over an unidentifiable lump of animalesque undercarriage.

'I'm here to show these boys your backyard, Benny,' said Chas.

The butcher's eyes flicked towards the rear exit.

'It isn't safe, Chas, you know that.' He lay down the cutlass and wiped the excess offal onto his apron. He knew that no matter how often he did this, he could never get the blood off his hands, it was too late for that, but it was a courtesy, for the children.

'Still, they need to see it,' said Chas. 'I won't let them get too close.'

Chas shuffled over to the rear exit and the boys followed him into a dank unlit storage area, shutting the butcher's shop away behind him. Blinks of sunshine licked between the cracks in the back door, saturating Chas's face with diffused light. It was as if he had become as young as them, that there were now four children, hearts pounding, standing on the brink of an adult world that did not deserve them.

When the door to the backyard was opened the boys were unable to take in what lay before them – they had no frame of reference.

'When the council built this city, there were the wisps and curls of other, smaller towns in the way of the bulldozers,' explained Chas. 'The local people were bought off quickly, they drank the Kool Aid and shut their eyes and when they had counted to ten, everything, the churchyards, the trees, the hedges, the rivers, the animals, everything, was concrete and no longer special and now those they abandoned are here – one on top of the other, on top of the other.'

Piled in the square at the rear of four giant, withered buildings, as high as the eye could see, were thousands upon thousands of gravestones, some smashed, some illegible, but many pristine, crypts – doors ajar, inverted angels, hands outstretched, eyes imploring as if this was some new, unforeseen depravity, beyond the travesty of death itself, everything that was loss was there, never to be forgotten but forgotten still. It was the lie told on the deathbed, that goodbye might only mean adieu, the final cogent evidence of betrayal.

And at its peak, where the angels could not reach and where a plateau had formed when the gravestones had settled, someone had made their home in a garden shed and on that garden shed was a sign in large, blood-red neon, flashing on and off, on and off: FUCK OFF (OR DIE).

Daniel had found his grandmother.

CHAPTER 38

Caldwell Bynes – the head teacher of D'Oily Cart Academy and a man who willingly accepted sole responsibility for the abject lack of educational prowess of generations of North London children – shifted uncomfortably in his exquisitely sumptuous chair, behind his insanely expensive antique desk. Wherever he looked, the horizon was filled to the brim with the deluge of adipose tissue and porcine corpulence that constituted M, Daniel's father.

'Will you stop gesticulating with that gun, you're making me nervous,' asked Bynes, not unreasonably.

'I want to know where my son is,' demanded M.

'He has become friends with Grellman and the odd child who wears two pairs of glasses and three watches.'

'Don't you know the other child's name?'

'I try not to know names – they just get in the way of really enjoying the day to day infliction of misery.'

'I thought Grellman was unable to make friends – I thought his sole purpose was dispensing senseless and arbitrary violence?'

'So did I but it appears that your son and the other child inadvertently saved his life. I am sure it will all work out for the best and he will rip them limb from limb – it's what he does best. Anyway the three of them have gone on a quest.'

'What do you mean "quest" – they aren't Jason and the fucking Argonauts, they are three eight-year-old boys.'

'Well, Grellman told me to close the school so they could go out for the day so I didn't really have any choice. I may be the manager of the zoo but I can't control what the residents of the insect house get up to.'

'Daniel is not an insect – he's my son.'

'That is a matter of perspective. Daniel believes you intend to kill him, M. He's telling anyone who will listen, which in truth, is not many people.' He studied the thirty-two stone policeman who was occupying both of the guest chairs in his office. His shirt was stuck to his tumescent gut by a mixture of acrid sweat and blood, the left arm of his uniform had been almost completely ripped off and he appeared to have used a bottle of human intestines as shampoo. 'Anyway, what does it matter to you where Daniel is? The whole trying to murder him repeatedly thing would not suggest a high degree of parental empathy.'

M moved with feline grace and lowered his cataclysmic stomach onto Bynes' desk. The desk made a sound not unlike the plaintive scream of a drone bee during the act of copulation, shortly after its penis has snapped off. It was not a sound that Bynes ever wanted to hear again.

'My twelfth birthday present from my father was a gun. I did consider shooting my mother who had been killing people for fun for some years, but I decided no, she may be a mass murderer but she's my mass murderer. My father on the other hand was the bitterest, most unremittingly poiso-nous fucker that had ever been vomited out onto this shitforsaken cesspit of a planet, so I put a bullet through his head at point blank range. It seems that the bullet missed his cerebral cortex but my mother decided it was better to dump me into foster care believing I had executed him. It wasn't until a few months ago when the old bastard turned up on my front door that I realised he wasn't dead. It also transpired that shooting him in the face had impacted on the quality of our relationship quite significantly.'

M dragged Bynes from his chair by his neck as if he were the weight of a glove puppet. Bynes found himself standing on his tiptoes with a gore-soaked gun waving like a metronome back and forth millimetres from his eyes.

'Don't lecture me about parental empathy, you cunt.' As he spat out this final word, aspirated blood sprayed from M's nose onto Bynes' face.

'Are you familiar with the story of Cassandra?' croaked Bynes. 'Her ears were licked clean by snakes enabling her to hear the future but she was cursed by Zeus so that no one would believe her predictions. She was shouting into a void like you, M – no one is listening. All these fucking children swarming around my feet like so many cockroaches and their parents bleating because Johnny can't fucking speak, James can't spell his own fucking name, James never stops crying, or Daniel won't die when I try to kill him. You're just like the rest of them, symptoms of the human disease – I hate the shitting lot of you.'

M released Bynes' throat from his grip and shifted around the desk, planting his foot between Bynes' legs. 'I intend to defenestrate you.'

Bynes stole a glance at his office window – painted closed – offering views of a playground occupied sporadically by children who experienced education as provocation, school as a battlefield, textbooks as graveyards.

'Well that's an interesting proposition, M, however you would be hard pressed to throw a child out of that window and God knows I've tried, let alone a fully grown adult.'

'That presupposes that you are in one piece when I do it, wouldn't you agree?' M pressed the nozzle of the gun into Bynes' nose, distending it.

'The more you threaten me the more I laugh at you,' replied Bynes with ill-considered defiance.

M burrowed the gun into Bynes' left nostril until his septum flayed and split. Bynes could tell this meeting was not going especially well.

'You are a sociopath, M.'

'I'm a fucking hero, Bynes, I'm what's stopping the swollen hordes of the unwashed who are massing outside the city gates with their torches and their boiling peat, from smashing down the walls of this Stickle Brick shit pile and murdering you and everyone like you while you are quivering under your Teenage Mutant Ninja Turtle quilts; I am the Grim Reaper and the tooth fairy; I am beauty and the beast; I am what England sees when it looks in the mirror.'

Bynes' fingers tiptoed into his desk drawer and caressed a letter opener into his grasp. He pulled away from M and swung his arm in an arc, plunging the blade into M's stomach. Both men looked down at the blade hanging out of M's gut. A blood bubble bloomed at the site of the wound and grew impossibly large before bursting, showering M's shirt with a fine spray of haemoglobin.

'I wish people would stop making holes in me,' said M, closing his hand over Bynes' nose and mouth without taking his eyes away from the wound. Bynes struggled, but his carousel pulled into the tunnel of love, never to emerge.

M began to laugh, 'I look like a pepperoni pizza,' which reminded him that he had not eaten for nearly twenty minutes. He decided to return home, order in a Chinese takeaway banquet, put on a Tom Jones CD and then he and his gun would sit and wait for Daniel.

CHAPTER 39

Chas walked over to the nearest marble angel of death, hanging down bat-like from the random construct of gravestones, tombs, guardians and watchers, and touched her cold outstretched hand. The huge statue and the funereal mountain it was part of wobbled alarmingly.

'You can't climb this because it will collapse and crush you,' said Chas, with as much authority as he could muster.

'And yet there must be a way,' said Dorsal.

'It's impossible, absolutely impossible,' sighed Daniel.

'Are you coming?' shouted Ferris, as his legs disappeared into a crypt that hung at a perilous angle twenty-five or more metres above their heads.

'I could have killed him, God knows I've had the opportunity,' grumbled Dorsal, cautiously placing his foot onto the head of a marble griffin. He reached out a hand with untypical largesse for Chas.

'I'm eighty-two'.

'And your point is?' asked Dorsal.

Chas took the bear's paw of a hand and Dorsal pulled him up and over his head onto the next funereal edifice. With every stuttering foothold Dorsal was at Chas's back, supporting him as if he were a toddler taking his first few steps for his father. Daniel followed just behind them. Dorsal's gentle behaviour was not a comforting vision – he reminded Daniel of the kind of animal that nurtures then eats its own young.

They found Ferris sitting on a caryatid in an art nouveau tomb. Dorsal used a leaded glass window as a foothold, pulling first Daniel and then Chas up with him. As he turned to face Ferris he noticed that his arrival had provoked a look of abject horror which even he found surprising. He quickly realised why – the entire tomb was capsizing backwards under their combined weight. Dorsal tried desperately to find a way to brace himself but the tomb was already beyond its tipping point and it began tumbling towards the ground far below.

*

'I have anticipated my death a hundred times before, only for it to be averted at the last moment. Eventually there is a sense that you have been cheated,' said Chas, separated from the abyss by Dorsal's fingertips which clung to his shirt collar.

Dorsal was hanging by his other hand from the wing tip of an angel and Ferris clung to his ears. The plaintive melody of human suffering that had been the theme tune to their ascent continued far above their heads where, in the shed that sat astride the funereal mountain, a man was screaming for mercy in a way that suggested he was not expecting to receive it.

Daniel was nowhere to be seen.

'If I manage to save your life and we get out of this, Ferris, I'm going to kill you,' growled Dorsal.

'You can't wage war against the entire world, Dorsal, you have to choose a side,' Ferris whispered.

'I just want to wage war against you, Ferris,' replied Dorsal.

Chas could feel Dorsal's grip on his collar loosen but he was not frightened for himself, only for the boys. They reminded him of his friends at school, always arguing about nothing, lost in the travails of youth before being torn to shreds by an enemy that treated them like annoying insects.

Ferris felt one of Dorsal's ears begin to unzip from its fastenings. Dorsal was losing his grip on the angel's wing.

'There is nowhere to go from here. What am I holding on for?' asked Dorsal.

'When we were waiting to die in the camp,' said Chas, 'waiting for the open door, the blank expression, the finger pointing towards the abyss, I asked myself where love had gone – had it drained away into the cracks between the planks in the floor beneath our lice-infested bunks, down into the deepest recesses of this planet from where it had once emerged? Was that what these places were for – a way to strip away the last vestiges of humanity, leaving us less than a mound of bones that were indistinguishable one from the other? I asked my father and my grandfather, was this ignominy really the end for all of us? I told them I had forgotten what hope looked like, we had been kept in the dark for so long that darkness was all we knew. My father did not have the words but my grandfather, the rabbi, told me that there was always a chance, that I should run if I had the slightest opportunity and never stop, the elbow in my cheek, the boot in my back, the bullet in my spine, nothing should stop me. If I escaped then all of my family would escape in me, if I were free, if they could see me be free, even for a split second then that would be a form of victory that would carry them through the end. I hated him for that, I wanted them to fight, to die fighting, clawing at the face of their enemy, but that was not in their design, they were great thinkers, but their hands would not form into fists.

'When they came, on the day that the last vestige of my humanity drained from my body, the door opened and I was through it, the butt of a gun hit me in the face but I kept on running like a headless chicken and they let me. Where was I going to? I was an ant whose kingdom had once seemed eternal, destroyed by the child with boiling water until everywhere I turned there was degradation. But I was quick and they saw that this mongrel, this odd Catholic Jew could be of use, that I was worth keeping alive for the moment. I was used to ferry messages from one part of the camp to another, from commandant to commandant, I was the fucking internet. To other Jews, I became a jinx. I was a rag doll, fighting with the German dogs for scraps from the table, I was more despised than the Kapos but I survived, when even the dogs died I survived and yet in so many ways I did not survive. My grandfather was wrong. I died with my family, hand in hand with them and what you see, the husk that remains, is indestructible but empty.'

And as Chas felt Dorsal's grip fail and gravity pulled him with her persistent grasp, he knew he could defy even her. He closed his eyes and prepared to fly like one of Chagal's winged horses.

CHAPTER 40

It took Chas more than a minute to open his eyes again and when he did so he realised that Daniel's grandmother, Bernice, had caught him and deposited him on the floor of another desecrated crypt beside Ferris and Dorsal. Viewing himself for a moment through her wicked eyes, Chas could see that to her the three of them were of no more importance than butterflies pinned behind a sheet of dusty glass.

'I was just climbing back up the ladder from the supermarket with my shopping, when I saw you clowns and decided I had better intervene before you drew any more attention to my little eagle's nest,' said Bernice.

'Yes, I saw that,' said Ferris, 'but the other route looked far more exciting.'

'You knew there was a fucking ladder and you didn't tell us. Right, that's it, I am going to actually rip your leg off and stick it up your arsehole.' Dorsal lurched towards Ferris but was prevented from reaching him because the slightly built sixty-year-old woman who had plucked him out of the air with Ferris still attached to his ears, appeared to have him in a half nelson. He thought he might be falling in love.

'What about Daniel?' Ferris enquired reluctantly.

'Oh I grabbed that and took it upstairs about ten minutes ago. It appeared to be relatively intact.'

*

Up in the shed, space was at a premium. Bernice had sectioned off a reception room, a bedroom and a bathroom/kitchen/conservatory/abattoir and every wall, every item of furniture, every square inch of flooring was decorated with dried and drying human blood and assorted detritus. It was a scene of singular, wretched desolation – much like McDonalds in Finsbury Park but without the plastic straws.

'I love what you've done with the place,' murmured Chas, searching forlornly for somewhere to sit which would not stain him permanently.

'Excuse me for just a second boys, I just have to pop next door and polish off a little unfinished business,' chirped Bernice.

There was a scrotum shrivelling howl before Daniel's grandmother re-emerged with the dripping severed head of the actor who had, until very recently, played Dr Who.

'This is just another example of the way in which TV lies to you boys, look and learn. They tell you these time lords regencrate after they die but I've beheaded three of the fuckers and they all stay as dead as this one.'

Daniel's grandmother waited with disappointment for a response but since her guests all appeared to be rigamortised with horror, she felt obliged to fill the conversational void.

'So what brings you to see your nana, Daniel? Forgotten the recipe for chicken soup?'

'My father wants to kill me – I love him but he just sees me as prey.'

'Love? Well you certainly didn't inherit that from our side of the family. Anyway, despising you seems reasonable enough. On the day you were born there was a game of pass the parcel and you and Saul had to fight for the last seat. Selfish of you, don't you think – leaving your sibling to die. You are clearly unfamiliar with the lyrics of The Hollies seminal 1969 number one, *He Ain't Heavy, He's My Brother.*'

'How can I be blamed? I was only a few seconds hold when he died.'

'Seems a little bit weak as excuses go.'

'I've come all this way, don't you have any advice for me?'

'You need to man up.'

'I'm eight and my thirty-two stone police sergeant father is trying to execute me and that's all you have to say?'

'You're lucky to get that, sunshine. Any grandson of mine should be able to look after himself. These three however, I can help.' She put down the severed head on the occasional table in front of them, went next door, popped back to turn the head round to face them and then came back again with a large, gore-soaked wooden chest.

'This is for you, six eyes,' she handed Ferris a huge sword/axe type weapon with two vicious spikes at either end. 'This is for you, elephant boy,' she gave Dorsal a large rectangular green metal box with 'property of US Army' written down the side. 'It's a rocket propelled grenade launcher,' she explained helpfully.

She walked over to Chas, took him by the hand and led him outside the shed, closing the door behind her. She pressed a small silk drawstring bag into his hand.

'This contains everything you are going to need,' said Bernice, 'six coins – one each for the boys' eyes – and a slip of paper on which I have written the Roman prayer for the dead; *Ego sum dea, mortua non sum.*'

'What about the weapons you gave them?' asked Chas.

'You could pitch up at 33 Bulstrode Avenue in the Starship fucking *Enterprise*, empty its entire array of photon torpedoes through the letterbox and it wouldn't even slow my son down.'

Chas stared at her with measured disgust. This woman was a different kind of evil…

'My son and I are not the bad guys.'

'That's like telling me to ignore the sinking *Titanic* and have sympathy for the iceberg,' said Chas.

'My husband told me I needed a hobby, I tried needlepoint and yoga but they didn't appeal, he was too busy knocking seventy shades of shite out of myself and our kids to understand the landscape he was painting. I know we may seem like monsters to you but that isn't even half the story.'

'If something looks like a vulture, smells like a vulture and acts like a vulture then it might as well be a vulture,' said Chas.

'We were the victims, my children and I. Somewhere in the space between the punches and the degrading abuse we were…set adrift.'

'And that justifies what you have done?' asked Chas. 'Is it somehow licence for that little boy's father to lay in wait, in his home, to end his life? You cannot abrogate all responsibility for the Gomorrah you have built.'

She took his right hand and placed it between her breasts – she was standing on the edge of the mountain. She held his left hand in hers. This was not tenderness, but it was all she had to offer.

'Can you please stop me? Stop me and perhaps, just perhaps you can stop him,' asked Bernice.

He felt her heart race.

'I cannot harm you, I am not equipped. It is not in my vocabulary.'

'If you could have put a stop to the carnage all those years ago, to the plunder of your family and friends, wouldn't you have done so, no matter how?'

He had often wondered.

He moved his right hand, it was no more than the tiniest of gestures but it was enough. She flew backwards and down and then she was gone.

From an early age death had surrounded him like a forest fire, leaving him with nowhere to hide, taking everyone and everything he cherished until love itself perished in the flames. Now he knew, finally, it was time to stop running and make a stand. If death wanted to take these three children it was going to have to get past him first.

CHAPTER 41

DCI Moses Waif was the commander of a crack police specialist firearms and hostage situations unit. 'I am the commander of a crack police specialist firearms and hostage situations unit,' he told the reflection in his bathroom mirror as he stood flicking the floss in and out of the gaps between his unruly teeth. He raised his left eyebrow and the corner of his mouth exactly twenty-five degrees (he had measured) and held them in place until he felt his cheek beginning to cramp. This was 'triumphant glare number 5' – it made him look steely and magnificent. 'I like it,' he told his reflection and his reflection liked it back. He was on top of his game.

He entered his kitchen which was glutted with child-related ephemera and picked his way to the best chance of sitting down the room had to offer, the top of an upturned filing cabinet. All chair-related surfaces had long ago been mandated for nappies – unused, ancient, full and any combination of the three. His two-year-old son Noah paused from his routine of throwing all food items from his high chair and then screaming for them to be returned, to dissect the man who purported to be his father with his blue-grey stare.

Moses sat down and excavated an inadequately small landing area for his cereal bowl, in a table that groaned under the weight of every cooking utensil and receptacle he and his wife had ever possessed, each one more debased with the remnants of culinary disasters.

Moses tried the 'triumphant glare number 5' on his son – a ray of sunlight played through the kitchen window and illuminated his face and he imagined that it made each of his features effervesce.

'I told you not to do that with your face, it scares the shit out of him,' snorted his wife Charon, as she blurred through the tiny room on the way to clean baby sick off her baby sick coloured blouse.

Moses searched his son's features but he stubbornly refused to resemble him in any way.

Minnow, their opulently disgruntled au pair, lurched into the kitchen, opened the fridge, took out the last carton of milk, drank it from the carton, swirled around the remaining dregs, drained these, held the carton up to the light to make certain that what remained was so insubstantial that it would prove insufficient to extract even the smallest essence of the DNA of the donating cow and put the empty carton back into the fridge.

Minnow was of indeterminate gender (it stated this on his/her application form for the job) and had a physique that was half-obese and half-anorexically thin. It wore a kimono and nothing else, which was often left alarmingly agape. Moses had never glimpsed the undercarriage which lay below, he feared it too much.

'What about a little bit of cleaning in here?' Moses asked with forced joviality.

Minnow stopped in the midst of a rapid flounce back in the direction of his/her room and launched his/her pupils into the roof of his/her head as if they were two tiny spacecraft. The following conversation was conducted with his/her back to Moses.

'I clin.'

'What do you clean?' demanded Moses, surveying a kitchen which appeared to showcase the total collapse of Western civilisation.

'I clin dis,' Minnow held up his/her mug which contained a drink which he/she made every morning and every evening that was of a greenish brown hue and was almost certainly toxic to humans.

'It's true,' intervened Moses' wife, now in a baby sick coloured suit, 'that cup has been cleaned to a subatomic level.'

'And I clean dis,' Minnow whisked up his/her kimono exposing an arse which glinted in the morning haze and exited the room.

Moses looked despairingly at his wife as she skimmed past him with her work case under one arm and a large pile of school exercise books against her right hip.

'If you want to change au pairs again, Moses, you will have to sack this one – good luck with that by the way – advertise for a new one and interview them, I haven't got time, I have to leave for school right now.'

He looked at Noah who was munching down on a huge rusk with stoic determination. 'Tell mummy what daddy does for a job, Noah.'

Noah's eyes brimmed with joy, he stopped mid chomp, put down the rusk carefully into a lake of dribble – this was the thing he did for daddy and he was proud of it.

'You de the colander of a crap piece of special flying pants and a goosey station.'

'Fuck me, our kid's a genius – shall we call *The Times*?' shouted Charon from the depths of their walk-in fridge.

'I don't see why it always has to be me who has to take time off work.'

'It's not as if you do anything important, Moses. I mean, shouting through a loudhailer, the occasional bit of ducking and shooting, anyone could do it.'

'Shooting people is important, Charon, especially if you're the person getting shot.'

'Yes yes, as I say, all very interesting but what do you actually achieve?'

'I negotiate with armed kidnappers in high pressure scenarios, I free hostages, I save lives, I make a difference.'

'And when's the last time you managed to do any of that? I thought your record this year was three sieges – no one saved, everyone dead. As I say, anyone can do that. You want to try explaining to a class of rabid ten-year-olds about why they should stop trying to set light to their geography teacher and come back to school to learn French, that's pressure, sunshine, not indiscriminately wiping out half of North London with big boys' toys.'

Moses' mobile rang – a call from DCI Minerva – and he was relieved to bring yet another one-sided argument with the most frightening woman in the world to an end.

'We've got a rogue policeman, Waif. He's already killed a bank robber, a junior officer and a headmaster. We need you to flush him out before the situation escalates. He's armed and he's wounded and he's the size of a bus.'

'I'm leaving now, Sir.' Moses assumed his 'I'm on a life or death mission' expression and stood up hurriedly.

'Oh, and Waif, try not to kill everyone this time.'

'Yes, Sir.'

Moses put on his bulletproof jacket and strode purposefully toward the door, his mind already awash with tactical stratagems and manpower synergies – he was a world beater.

'Where the fuck do you think you're going, sunshine?' Charon had put on her coat and held a case brimming with exam papers.

'I've got to go. There's a situation that needs my tactical assault team.'

'Not before you empty the dishwasher and change Noah,' said Charon.

She gave him the kind of look which Medusa employed to turn men to stone, ruffled his hair, kissed Noah and strode out of the house.

*

It is difficult to really appreciate the finer points of a meal consisting of a thirty-six piece Chinese feast, a family-sized quattro formaggi pizza and a whole Tandoori chicken, when you are bleeding to death. It was not that M had lost his galactic appetite, it was more that food which is covered in your own plasma all tastes the same after a while.

M had tried to patch his wounds with the tiny sticking plasters that he had found at the back of his bathroom cabinet but after experimenting with other objects, found that the only effective method of staunching the flow was gaffer taping half a dozen copies of *Playboy* over the entry sites.

He sat in his favoured green velour armchair and turned the gun over and over in his hands. Its cold weight was reassuring. He pointed the gun towards the front door and dug around in the allotment of his memories to unearth Daniel's face, but he could not retrieve it. He could not remember the face of his son and he needed to remember it if he was going to erase it and him forever.

CHAPTER 42

Moses lay on his stomach, the damp undulating tarmac of the road outside M's home a reassuring presence. He clenched and unclenched his abs, threw back his shoulders, adjusted the lapels of his bulletproof jacket, swept his dirty blond hair out of his eyes and imagined how he must appear to Stables and Thorn, the police marksmen who lay beside him under the cover of their armoured police vehicle.

'I think of myself as Odysseus,' whispered Moses, 'fighting and defeating the Cyclops against all the odds, an indefatigable warrior on a legendary mission.'

Thorn looked up from his rifle sight and into Moses' eyes. Moses felt that his expression conveyed more than respect – perhaps even adoration.

'There's a police dog pissing on your legs,' said Thorn, returning his eye to the rifle sight.

'Fucking little, fuck…' screamed Moses and as he did so, his head shot upwards, smashing into the armoured vehicle and then down, directly into a pool of dog piss.

'Awe inspiring,' muttered Thorn.

*

In the house, M had emptied a bladder so capacious that it would have given a water buffalo an inferiority complex and was just leaving the bathroom when he caught sight of movement under one of the cars parked in front of the house. He immediately recognised it as an unmarked armoured police vehicle, pulled back from the window as if he had been slapped in the face and glimpsed his face in the bathroom mirror – it was contorted into a silent scream.

'Fuck, fuck fuck fuck.' M pulled the gun out of his pocket, put the barrel in his mouth, pulled the safety off and shut his eyes. He pulled it out, looked at his face again, his watermelon head rolling about on his shoulders as if it was no longer attached and pushed the gun back in again, breaking off one of his front teeth in the process. He tried to pull the trigger but it was as if his fingers were made of sponge. He spat out the gun, threw it on the floor and stared at his anguished, tormented expression in the mirror. He wailed his first name, 'shit-fuck-bastard,' before smashing his face into the glass.

*

Moses was still trying to shake the dog piss out of his ears when his radio began spewing out static-laden words. It was Crown, who was the leader of his B team and had been instructed to cover the other side of M's house.

'In place, Sir. We have the building in lockdown.'

'Excellent work, Crown. Can you see any movement?'

'Nothing really, Sir, just a cat having a crap in the garden.'

'Funny that,' pondered Moses, 'there's a white cat having a crap in the garden in front of us as well.'

A thought buzzed around Moses' head, he tried to swat it away but it was doggedly persistent. It was not a thought he liked.

'What else can you see, Crown?'

'Well, Sir…'

Moses turned to his left to find Crown lying on the ground under a second armoured response vehicle about ten metres away.

'I can see you, Sir.'

Moses scrambled to his feet and ensuring he trod mightily on Crown's groin, sprinted towards the side road which led to the back garden of M's house.

*

When M heard the back door open he assumed it was the police tactical response team and tore down the stairs holding the gun in front of him, fully prepared for a final deadly confrontation. He was surprised to find Daniel standing in the kitchen with a small boy who wore two pairs of glasses and a rictus grin, an elderly man who was dressed like a commando and a child who appeared to be the size of a small elephant.

M raised the gun, removed the safety and pointed it at Daniel. In response, Dorsal pointed the grenade launcher at M, Ferris raised the huge double pointed axe over his head and Chas pointed what looked like a vacuum cleaner hose pipe at M.

M was not at his best, pieces of glass hung from his shredded face where he had smashed it into the mirror, his upper torso was covered in gore-soaked pornographic magazines which had been gaffer taped in place and blood was running down both of his legs and pooling onto the ground around his feet.

'Hi, Dad, I'm home,' murmured Daniel.

'Nice to meet you, Mr M,' chirped Ferris, his arms shaking under the tremendous weight of the axe.

'Anyone fancy a glass of cola or some crisps?' enquired M. His left hand was developing an involuntary twitch and he knew that sooner rather than later this was going to spread to his right hand and more specifically his trigger finger. He felt faint and nauseous and yet everything in the room was pin sharp.

'Not for me thanks, Mr M,' said Dorsal, who had aimed the grenade launcher at M's head and armed it to fire.

'Surely I can offer you a nice cup of tea and a biscuit?' M nodded towards Chas without taking his eyes off Daniel.

'Nice of you to offer but aren't you a little busy?' asked Chas.

'Oh, it's no trouble, I'll pop the kettle on then, shall I?' replied M, fumbling behind himself whilst still fixed on Daniel and flicking on the plug socket, leaving a bloody fingerprint on the wall in the process. 'I just need to kill my son first if you don't mind.'

Dorsal pressed the trigger of the grenade launcher and nothing happened. He turned it round to reread the instructions on the side when the weapon engaged and sent a fully armed grenade smashing through the kitchen window where it continued happily on its way before exploding some distant and presumably innocent subject.

Ferris tried to wield the axe at M but in his efforts to hold it above his head, his pipe cleaner-thin arms dropped down and he could no longer find the strength to lift it more than an inch off the ground.

M smiled as his finger closed on the trigger, until Chas smacked the vacuum cleaner hose pipe directly into his nose, causing M to fling the gun across the kitchen.

There was a moment of perturbed stillness during which both men felt like they were under water and as M followed the scuttering trajectory of the gun, he was surprised to see it come to rest beside a woman's patent leather shoe.

'Leave my son alone, you fat fuck pig,' hissed Daniel's mother, who had emerged from the walk-in larder seconds before with a familiar spade which was already arcing towards M's skull.

CHAPTER 43

Moses had just entered M's back garden when the kitchen window exploded and a rocket-launched grenade whistled gracefully towards his face.

'Fucking my old boots,' shrieked Moses, eloquently summarising his situation and managing to duck just sufficiently for the grenade's trajectory to take it not between his eyes but down his centre parting.

Turning as if inebriated, Moses watched the grenade hit a letterbox, which shot up into the stratosphere like a missile until plummeting down again into the back of a milk float.

Moses was standing transfixed in a snowstorm of milky glass when Stables and Thorn arrived. Stables looked from the milk float to M's kitchen window and then back at Moses. 'Your hair is on fire, Sir,' proffered Stables. 'I know,' replied Moses, 'I know.'

*

M managed to block and hold the shank of the shovel before his wife was able to stove his head in with it. There was a brief period of grappling before Daniel's mother let go of the shovel, partly because M was too strong for her and partly because Daniel, who was now holding the gun, had placed it against her stomach.

'What are you doing, Daniel?' she asked.

'I'm bringing this to an end,' replied Daniel, walking over to his father and handing the gun back to him.

'I don't understand,' said his mother, who was hugging herself and shuffling from the light to the dark kitchen tiles and back again in a one woman waltz.

'You haven't earned the right to understand, Mum. Good or bad – at least M has been a father to me. You, you just faded away.'

M was examining the gun as if he had never seen it before. 'This changes nothing,' he said to no one in particular, raising the gun once again like an automaton.

'Would you mind standing aside while I blow your father to pieces?' asked Dorsal patiently. He had reloaded the grenade launcher and was keen to try it out again. He was definitely going to use this in the playground – a weapon like this would raise his credibility as a bully to hitherto unimaginable levels.

Daniel stood directly in front of his father.

'Not until I have the answers to some questions,' replied Daniel.

'Well, if it's answers you want,' said M, grabbing Daniel and planting the barrel of the gun diagonally into the top of his head, 'then ask away before I decorate this room with your central nervous system. But bear in mind that this will be a conversation which ends with the "b" in bang.'

*

Moses, Thorn and Stables had advanced to the bush at the end of M's garden. Moses had extinguished his hair and Stables and Thorn had trained their rifles on the kitchen.

'I have a kill shot, Sir,' said Thorn, 'do I have your permission to take it?'

'Is it a clean shot, Thorn – is his son clear?' Moses asked.

'I thought the child was the target, Sir, I distinctly read that in the briefing note that....Not kill the child. Really?'

Moses inhaled so much air that his lungs were on the point of exploding and turned to Stables. There was neither hope nor expectation in his voice when he spoke.

'What about you?'

'I can't get a clean shot of M, Sir, there are too many people in the way.' He paused. 'We could just shoot everyone.'

Moses sucked a thoughtful tooth, grabbed the rifle from Stables and ran down the garden towards the kitchen door. If there was going to be carnage here he wanted it to be his kind of carnage.

*

'So why kill me, kill your surviving son, what will that achieve?' asked Daniel.

'This was never about you, Daniel. It was about failure – it was about holding your brother's body in my arms and being unable to make him be alive again, no matter how tightly I held him, how hard I begged and begged him to breathe. It was about kissing each one of his tiny fingers one last time and knowing that when I let go, someone was going to take him away from me and bury him in the ground. More than anything, it was about losing his smile, the smile he gave as a gift to me and only me. It was a smile that lit me up and losing it extinguished a flame that could never, ever be reignited.'

'And your solution was violence?' asked Daniel.

'Violence is an elegant language punctuated by fear. It was the way I communicated after they took your brother from me.'

Daniel's mother was touching the top of the kettle now in sets of five, five was important, five made her laugh and cry and scream and vomit but it had to be repeated and repeated. 'I drove through a supermarket and killed your son, blame me. If you are going to kill someone then kill me.'

'How can I kill you when you died in that accident?' asked M. 'I can't see you, can't feel you, you don't exist.'

*

Moses could see that the situation in the kitchen was rather tricky, that the wrong decision would result in devastation on a biblical scale. He threw himself against the wall to the side of the kitchen door and lifted his walkie-talkie to his mouth.

'Is your attack team in place, Crown?'

There was a brief static hiatus.

'All in place, Sir,' whispered Crown. 'We will smash in the front door, enter the house through the hallway and take out M in the kitchen. Ready to go on your mark.'

'All in place outside the front door of number 22?' enquired Moses.

More static. Moses could just make out the word 'bollocks.'

*

'How is any of this Daniel's fault?' asked Daniel's mother, who was now frenziedly touching the kettle with alternate hands and her forehead. A line of drool leached from the corner of her mouth.

'From the first moment I saw him I knew he wasn't his brother, could never replace his brother,' said M. 'I hated him for that, will always hate him for it. His face is not quite his brother's, his voice is not quite his brother's voice and when I held his hand for the first time...'

Daniel looked up at his father, turned, wrapped his arms around his father's wretched bloody waist and hugged him. He hugged him and he cried because he couldn't be brave any more. And as he cried so did Dorsal, for the mother and father that had betrayed him. And as Dorsal cried so Ferris cried for the father he had lost until the end of his days. And as Ferris cried, Chas cried for the brutal loss of his innocence and the child he still remained, finding himself once again fighting with the dogs for survival.

Just as Moses kicked in the kitchen door and raised his weapon to fire on M, Daniel's mother swung the kettle into M's head with such deadly force it felled him like a mighty oak that would never rise again.

And before he fell, just for a few seconds, Daniel had felt M hug him back.

ACKNOWLEDGEMENTS

I would like to thank the following people:

My wonderful wife Catherine who has supported me unquestioningly every step of the way as she always does. The incredible Tony Cook, the creator and driving force behind ABCtales, without whose encouragement and support, very simply, this book would not exist. Matthew Marland for the first edit of the book. Luke Neima who is not only the nicest man on the planet but who re-edited and inspired and nursed this book towards its final form. Everyone at ABCtales but in particular Peter Hitchen (Scratch), Claudine Lazar, Richard Penny, Jolono for constantly encouraging me to continue writing and laughing at all the right bits of the story. My family and friends including my sisters Simone and Jackie, the sublime Fiona and Candice back at the office and in particular Sam my nephew and Marsha my cousin who harassed everyone they had ever known to pledge on a daily basis and who were there for me whenever I flagged. Isobel and the wonderful team at Unbound whose professionalism and high standards ensure that Unbound is synonymous with quality.

Finally, in the process of raising money for Shooting Star Children's Hospice as part of the pledging process I came find out a little more about this unique resource for life-limited children. Please look at their website and donate.

SUBSCRIBERS

Unbound is a new kind of publishing house. Our books are funded directly by readers. This was a very popular idea during the late eighteenth and early nineteenth centuries. Now we have revived it for the internet age. It allows authors to write the books they really want to write and readers to support the writing they would most like to see published.

The names listed below are of readers who have pledged their support and made this book happen. If you'd like to join them, visit: www.unbound.co.uk.

Ola Aderinola
Sami Aknine
Richard Alomo
Maame Ama Ntiwaah
Anonymous!
Rebecca Atkinson
Alan Austin
Tom & Jean Austin
Catherine Avadis
Rosalind Avadis
Andrew Bagchi
Jay Banerji
David Bannocks
Bertie Barget-Bluestone
Erin Barnes
Adrienne Barnett
Steven Bastien
Merlin Batchelor

Jane Berthoud
Judy Bishton
Christina Blacklaws
Brian Bloom
Fiona Bloom
Jerome Bloom
Paul Bloom
Simone Bloom
Oliver Breckon
Peter Breckon
Nicholas Bridgman Baker
Michael Brierley
Lizzie Brind
Simon Brind
Tricia Brind
Alison Brooks
Roger Brooks
Simon Brooks

Rory Brown
Jamie Byrne
Rowan Caffull
Xander Cansell
Geoff Carr
Joseph Caulfield
Alex Ching
Beryl Claydon
David Clayton
Michael Cogan
Ivor Cohen
Stevyn Colgan
Eric Compton
Francesca Conn
Joan Connell
Jason Conway
Tony Cook
Jeanette Covington
John Crawford
Andrew Croker
Joe Curl
Marcia D. Miller
Sudeepta Dasgupta
Minesh Davda
Sumner Davenport
Chris Davidson
Louise Davies
Lloyd Davut
Robert Day
Edward Denehan
Diana Dobson
Mark Donegan
Richard Drew
Francois Dumonteil-Lagreze
Michael Durham
Mark Edward Pearson-Freeland
Jackie Evans
Kim Evans
Samantha Evans

Robert Fairley
David Farmbrough
Graham Fewell
Mark Fletcher
Monica Ford
Isobel Frankish
Stephen Friel
Julia Furley
Simon Gale
Clare Gaskin
Anthony George
Michael Gero
Malcolm Gordon
Carrie Griffiths
David Griffiths
Lona Haddadi
Sophie Hall
Inzar Haq
Jill Harris
Daniel Harry
Caitlin Harvey
Ben Hayward
David Herbert
Andrew Heron
Lisa Hinsley
Peter Hitchen
Saira Hoda
Angela Hodgkinson Yorke
Ruth Horton
Denise Hyams
Sally Ibbotson
David Jaffe
David Jockelson
Graham Johnson
Malcolm Johnson
Daniel Jones & Magda DuPreez
Karen Jones
Marie José Nieuwkoop
Ian Joyner

Akiva Kahan	Kevin O'Brien
Elsie Katz	Anne Oakes
Rita Kaufman	Maureen Obi-Ezekpazu
Michael Kaye	Michael Pan
Karen Keating	Carolyn Pearson
Paula Kelly	Andy Pegg
Caroline Kennedy	Richard Penny
Sara Ketteley	Isabella Perner
Dan Kieran	Keith Phillips
Mark Kilburn	Deborah Piccos
Kanchanmala Kumar	Roy Pickering
Ray Lakeman	Andrew Pillidge
Henry Lamb	Lee Playle
Kate Lamont	Justin Pollard
Trevor Lang	Simon Pottinger
Katie Law	Neil Pretty
Joe Lawrence	Nigel Priestley
Ewan Lawrie	Anthony Raumann
Claudine Lazar	Judy Raumann
Stephen Lewis	Kiran Rcyat
Carole Lindsay-Scott	Helen Richardson
Nigel Lipton	Candice Rochford
Caroline Little	Moya Rooke
Jo Locker	Neil Rosenbaum
Hannah Markham	Neil Russell
Adrian Mars	Olusola Samuel Aina
Carolyn Martin	Richard Samuel
Richard McConnell	Tabasum Sarfraz
Ian McCormack	Andrew Shaw
Karen McDonnell	Helen Shaw
Kirsten McNamara	Emma Sherrington
Jacky Medway	Emily Shipp
Martin Michaels	AJ Singh
Christopher Miller	Rachael Smart
Wai Ming Loh	Carlos Solomon
Geoffrey Mott	Xenia Stavrou
Chris Ness	Damian Stuart
Rob Newlyn	Douglas Taylor
Jack O'Donnell	Adam Thomas

Mallory Towers
Greg Turnbull
Phyllis Turvill
Renate Van Workum
Louis Victor
Marisa Victor
Peter Victor
VyVy
Kiri Walden
Paul Walton
Mark Warwick

Sarah Weatherley
Eveline Wee
Jackie Wilson
Roger Wilson
Sam Wilson
Daniel Winson
Vikki Withrington
Gary Yau
Naomi Yeshua
Martin Young